PREVIOUSLY USED
Second Time Around For These Horror Stories

Edited by Dorothy Davies

PREVIOUSLY USED
Second Time Around For These Horror Stories

GRAVESTONE PRESS

CONTENTS

The Beggar – Dan Allen

Out Of The Frying Pan - Chris Rodriguez

Laughter In A Jugular Vein -Terrance V Mc Arthur

The Dragon Detector – Elana Gomel

Empty Nest – Sarah Townend

Deadly Masquerade – Chris Marchant

Il Migliore del Mondo – Alaric Cabiling

Inside The Walls - Chris Rodriguez

Chrysalis - Robert Allen Lupton

A Lonely Place – Dorothy Davies

Blinding A Few Dogs – Gary Budgen

Rent Money – Rie Sheridan Rose

Becoming Witch – Olivia Arieti

Little Dove – Donna L Greenwood

To Run Is To Fly – Rie Sheridan Rose

Above the Ceiling – Dan Allen

Dreams of Duality – Dorothy Davies

Lost and Damned – Olivia Arieti

The Lute Woman – Sheree Shatsky

Bobby Bumping – Diane Arrelle

First Fruits – Chris Rodriguez

Love Letters – S J Townend

Payback's A Bitch – Leslie Gulvas

Tiny Fridge – Sheree Shatsky

Death Wish – Edward Ahern

The Bad Ones Are Always The Best – Michelle Ann King

Where Only The Mosquitoes Sing – Dan Allen

The Day Death Wore Boots – Dorothy Davies

The Beggar

Dan Allen

He sits cross-legged on the sidewalk. There is a chill in the cement, but the air is warm and the sun has finally come back from months of winter. People pass by but don't see him. Crowds subconsciously change their path to avoid him. His back is getting uncomfortably warm and he wants to take off his jacket, but it's part of his uniform. So are his aviator sunglasses. He takes pleasure in staring at them. The oblivious hordes, hurrying about. He doesn't want them to see his eyes. He doesn't want them to see where he stares. His empty coffee cup sits in front of him, part of his uniform. It is to collect the change they drop in. Its bigger purpose is to complete the illusion.

***

Teri looks in the mirror. She is gorgeous and knows it, but she thinks everyone is beautiful. Everyone knows Teri and everyone loves her. She makes friends easily and holds friends dear. She comes from a small town where she attended the local college. She is not overly interested in boys. She dates a few but never for long. Boys are for later when she's ready to get married and have a family.

***

7

His hands are filthy and his fingernails packed with dirt. His pants appear stained from a hundred wine spills and perhaps many nights sleeping in puke. Passersby don't look close enough to see it's not real. There's no printed sign in front of him. He doesn't bother with one. Yet, to the unsuspecting crowd, it's obvious why he is there.

He deliberately sits in the centre of the sidewalk. He likes the view as they absentmindedly walk around him. The closer they get, the better. With spring in the air, it is unwrapping season—harvest time for his prodding eyes. Long coats and boots replaced with pantyhose and high heels. He feels a stirring.

***

Teri got by in school, finished college and moved to the big city. She isn't passionate about pursuing further education. Teri only wants to be with her friends, share time with them, travel, explore the world and shop. She has a wonderful fashion sense. The girl has never worn a pair of blue jeans in her life. She prefers skirts and dresses. She likes high heels instead of sneakers.

***

He keeps the empty coffee cup close but not because someone might snatch it. And he isn't worried that it will get kicked over. The coffee cup collects the coins, but it's also a lure. It draws them in close. He watches their legs, their shapes and

8

curves. From his street-level vantage point, he can often see up the thighs. He can imagine the rest. He sits on the cement for that very reason. Begging for money is not his primary purpose. He is hunting.

***

People don't see Teri as a snob. She is kind and generous and has friends from all walks of life. Teri doesn't see herself as naive, but she is. She is far too trusting. The girl believes bad things may happen to other people but never to her. Teri travels the city streets with the same fearless innocence she has when she travels the world.

***

He says nothing when someone contributes their silver. He doesn't look in when the coins hit the cup and he doesn't count them. The money doesn't matter and he doesn't say thank you. They don't make eye contact and they don't see who he watches, where he looks. The sunglasses are there to make sure. Girls don't notice when he allows a small smile to escape the corner of his mouth.

***

She has an office job in the city. She has a basement apartment in the suburbs and commutes. Teri smiles whenever she hears the old BTO song about *taking the 8:15 into the city*. That's her song, her motto, "takin' care of business". Work hard and play

9

harder, right? Teri likes her office job. She enjoys dressing up for work and wearing fancy clothes. Teri thinks her life is perfect.

***

The men are disgusted by him; the ladies fear him. He is dirty, but the ladies are what he desires. They are the ones most likely to fill his cup. He smiles as he thinks about their guilty need to give money to street people. It pleases him to know that they would be horrified if he were to touch them. They do not see him smile. He is invisible. An old hag walks over. Even to him, she is hideous. She is bending over, trying to hand him something. It is a Jesus pamphlet. He will not take it. She is blocking his view. He wants her gone. She stuffs the leaflet in his coffee cup. He silently curses her as she wanders off to save someone else. She ruins his day.

***

Today Teri brought home a kitten. She always laughed at crazy cat people and now she knows she is one. Teri names the cat "Pounce". She likes the name because it is simple. Pounce has an annoyingly cute way of laying upside down, paws in the air, watching Teri move about. They stay together at night. Pounce claws up under the blankets and burrows around until she falls asleep.

***

Their legs are at eye level to his stare and he watches them all, coming and going. He sees the curves and he prefers seeing them from behind. He allows his eyes to wander up to their ass. Don't they know he can see their asses? Spandex and Tights are okay, bare legs are better, but the Holy Grail is a pair of high heels and pantyhose. He likes them black with a pattern running up the back. He picks them out of the crowd. He discreetly sniffs as they pass.

***

Teri ran out of cat food, so now she feeds Pounce tuna. Pounce is finicky and it will be tuna only from now on. Teri does not mind. Tuna costs the same. Teri goes to bed and lets Pounce drink water from a Dixie cup. Teri thinks about what she will wear to work in the morning. The girl has two closets stuffed with clothes. The weather has been warming up and she is thinking about breaking out some of her spring pretties.

***

He gets ready for the day. He never shaves. It is part of the look. He pulls on his ripped, grease-covered jeans, a few layers of torn shirt and nasty running shoes. His baseball cap and, of course, his sunglasses. It's been a month since his last selection and the urge is growing strong. Finally, it's time to choose.

He takes his position—a rowdy group of boys approach—baseball fans, perhaps. One of them throws pocket change at him. The coins miss the cup and scatter. The young lads laugh, possibly expecting to see a bum scamper around chasing quarters. But he does not move. Instead, he bites his lip to contain his rage. He wants to rip these assholes apart and lets out a low growl. The boys don't hear it, but perhaps they sense something is wrong with this picture and they quickly move along.

Something delicious approaches and he lowers his sunglasses. He sees milky white legs, bare and flawless. The girl has a frisky bounce in her step, almost teasing. She gets closer and he stops breathing... She is not the one. Too young. She is just starting to bud. He will give her time to ripen—a prospect. For a second, he smiles.

***

Teri strolls towards the commuter trains. She is thinking about making Guacamole.

***

He spotted her today. She might as well have had a giant neon sign floating above her head. His radar picked her up before she even crossed the street. Her walk was just right. She moved slowly with confidence. Her skirt was short and her legs went on forever. He could see better now, black pantyhose indeed! He rattles his cup as she nears, hoping to get her attention. Just a momentary pause. Just enough to smell her. She doesn't miss a step and her pace remains the same. Her mind undoubtedly elsewhere. He breaks protocol and turns his head to watch her walk towards the trains, to follow the black pantyhose with a simple line running up the back. He tingles.

***

Teri is in the shower. The girl hears a noise and it freaks her out. She is paranoid and the splashing water drowns out her ability to tell if someone is there. She holds her breath as she grabs the faucet. She pauses and considers that once she turns off the water, the intruder will be on alert. Screw it; she turns off the water and hears a yowl. It is a long sorrowful cry. Forget drying off, Teri sticks her head out the bathroom door. She is naked and dripping water everywhere. It's only Pounce. She has one of her toys in her mouth. It is a small stuffed animal and the cat is carrying it around like it is her dead baby, howling out a mournful cry. As soon as Pounce sees Teri, she drops the dead baby and her crying ends. Teri wonders what else Pounce does when she thinks she is alone. Strange frigging cat.

***

He sees her at least once a day, twice if he gets out early enough. She always crosses in the late afternoon, merging with the sea of spawning people swimming upstream to the commuter trains. He has given up trying to get her attention. She passes him every single day and doesn't appear to notice him. He will make sure she sees him soon, but not today.

The authorities have never questioned him and he fits no profile. He is invisible even to the police. There are no reasons for his method. He hides in plain sight. He hunts in plain sight. If the ladies could see his eyes, they would see the lust, but his sunglasses do their job.

He sees her coming. Can he really smell her from where he sits? He believes so. He raises his head and watches her approach. This is not in character. He needs to keep his face down, but he can't help himself and he breaks his own rules. She passes on his right, dark nylons, no lines, but killer high heels. He can see firm muscles on the back of her legs, on her calves. Once she passes, he moves quickly. In one continuous movement, he sheds a few layers of filth and slides these excess clothes and the coffee cup into the first trash can he sees. He doesn't need this uniform anymore. He will make a new one next time. He smiles, already thinking about another hunt.

He jogs to catch up and falls in a dozen bodies behind her. He is confident and prepared. The commuter trains only run east and west. She goes through the westbound gate and gets on the first car. He pauses, watching through the windows, tracking to see where she sits. He climbs on board and picks a spot several rows behind her. He doesn't stand out and nobody seems to notice him. The glasses prevent eye contact.

14

On the streets thirty minutes later, he sees her enter the side door leading to what must be a basement apartment. He allows himself a rare teeth exposed smile. Her residence is ideal and he heads home. He will sleep well tonight. It will be an early morning.

***

Teri enters her apartment and instantly feels eyes on her. It's that creepy feeling she gets when someone is watching. She turns quickly to see a furry face. Perched on top of a bookshelf, Pounce controls the highest point in the room. Teri calls her a little bastard. Pounce lets out a soft meow and jumps down. The cat circles Teri's legs, looking for food. Teri relents and grabs a can of tuna.

***

Today he will not be on the streets. He has made his choice and knows exactly where she lives. He puts on a different uniform. Clean jeans, shirt and shoes. Neutral colours. He looks like anybody. He will blend in. Something silver and sharp replaces the coffee cup. The sunglasses remain the same. It is early dawn and he watches from the bushes. A light comes on.

***

Teri is already awake before her alarm goes off. Pounce has been nudging her for the past hour. Teri is a morning person and she plays a game of finger mouse with Pounce before jumping out of bed and heading to the bathroom. Pounce follows her, perhaps looking for soft food. Teri is high ponytail happy. She is looking forward to brushing her teeth and having a shower.

***

He sees another light come on in a small window, probably the bathroom and it's showtime. He steps out from the shadows of the shrubbery and moves quickly to the side door. The shower is his telltale sign. He relishes the way the noise from the cascading water muffles his approach. He loves how the steam-filled room blurs any movement. Most of all, he loves how the warm shower relaxes and sedates his prey.

***

Teri closes her eyes as the first streams of water engulf her head. It feels wonderful. She enjoys bathing and being naked. She always needs to be clean. She throws her head back to allow the spray to roll down her face and she hears something. Her heart skips a beat. Is there someone inside her apartment? Teri decides it's only Pounce and relaxes. She soon loses herself in the steam.

***

He is just outside the door and hears the pounding of the water on the tile floor and the lid snap on the shampoo. He hardens. It excites him that she has no idea he is there.

Teri comes back from a daydream and turns off the taps. The house is quiet. She has taken too long and is running late. She hurries to dry off. She throws open the door and catches movement from the side. Fear paralyses her. She feels betrayed by the shower for leaving her so vulnerable.

***

He flinches as the door whips open. She only has a towel wrapped around her waist. Her hair is wet and beads of water roll down her breasts. She smells clean and he pauses a moment to take in the perfection. Fear drips from her eyes, it's too stimulating and he loses control. He lunges incredibly fast. The knife sinks in, over and over again.

Out of the Frying Pan

Chris Rodriguez

Maybe this is a big mistake, thought Shelly. Her stomach churned, not because the flight to Taiwan bumped through turbulence, but because she wondered if living in a foreign country would solve her problems.

She yawned and looked behind her where Mr. Bedford was sitting. He smiled in reassurance. Shelly looked at his wife sleeping next to him. *Mrs. Bedford looks quite a bit older than Mr. Bedford. Whatever does he see in her?* Still, she was nice and Shelly felt they could get along.

She wondered how they had convinced her father to let her go overseas for a year even as such an important person as Mr. Bedford's lab assistant. Dad finally consented after being assured that his daughter would receive the best private education, though Shelly suspected that her stepmother, who hated her, had been the swing vote.

Shelly didn't fit in at her school either, but scholastically was far above her senior grade levels. She excelled at science and math and quickly developed a crush on her science teacher who acknowledged her natural abilities. He groomed her as his personal assistant. She corrected the other students' papers and took over when Mr. Bedford needed to leave. The others despised her, especially the girls who watched his every move with big doe eyes and wet lips. His dark exotic looks intoxicated them. Shelly, however, denied that she had that kind of a crush. She loved him for his mind. He was more intelligent and sophisticated than the other teachers and was always willing to listen when she felt sad and unloved.

Mr. Bedford was the only person she could talk to when her mother died suddenly and her father remarried a much younger woman within the year. She believed she would do anything to get out of that place. Shelly had run away several times but was always found. Her father would then ground her, like it wasn't punishment enough just being stuck with that bitch. Once reprieved, she would then take another "vacation" from the battlefield her father and his wife called home. She couldn't stand confinement.

Shelly sighed in contentment, wiping away the cobwebs of doubt. He had chosen *her* to come and help in his research. She was going to enjoy every minute of it. Afterward, she would be off to college and would never return to her father's internment camp. *I can't wait*, she thought.

Two hours later the flight attendant announced their landing. The deplaning was hectic as everyone moved swiftly around her. She appreciated Mr. Bedford's steady hand guiding her along the crowded platform. Mrs. Bedford took her other arm and together they traversed the concourse. As the threesome rounded a corner near the Baggage Claim, the adults tightened their hold on Shelly and steered her sharply to the left. Shelly looked up at them, questioning. Mr. Bedford nodded at her in silent encouragement.

A few minutes later they entered a new concourse where two Asian men approached them. They said something to Mr. Bedford in pidgin and he answered back gruffly. Shelly heard the words, "Watch... runner... your problem now." The men stepped away and Mrs. Bedford went with them. They chatted quietly nearby as Mr. Bedford guided Shelly over to a corner where he looked directly into her eyes. He wasn't smiling now.

What's wrong? Shelly wondered.

"You will be going with these men now, Shelly."

"But I thought I was going with you!" Shelly was consumed with anxiety. She didn't know who those men were. She felt a churning, sinking feeling in her stomach as she glanced at them. She didn't like the way they stared at her.

"You will go with them and you will do what they tell you," Mr. Bedford said sharply as he squeezed her upper arm. Then he relaxed his grip and smiled tightly at her. "Look," he told her, "They will bring you to the lab in a couple of days. I need time to set up."

"Promise?" Shelly asked still confused and more than a little worried.

"Sure," he said. "Don't worry about it." He walked her over to the men who handed him a thick envelope. She saw Mr. Bedford take something out of the envelope and hand it to Mrs. Bedford who tucked it in her bag.

The strange men stepped up on each side of Shelly and took her arms tightly. "We go this plane now," the shorter one said in broken English.

20

She struggled a bit as she looked back for her trusted teacher. He had gone without so much as a wave. She felt a sting as one of the men stuck a needle into her arm.

Wait! Her mind issued a silent scream. *I want to go home!*

Laughter In A Jugular Vein

Terrance V. Mc Arthur

What could bring over seventy five vampires to the same building in the middle of the night?

It had to be something bad.

The V-team secured the perimeter. Phillips and Rieker watching the doors. Wendy across the street with night-vision goggles and a clear view of the rooftop. My job: recon— penetrate the building, get the lay of the place, identify the location of the targets and report back to Team Leader. Fred: wouldn't choose him as being in charge of anything more involved than a hot dog wagon, but he's the guy who started the team and he had the van, so he was the boss of the Vampire Identification Project, the V.I.P.

Vampire Identification Project. The name seems kind of silly, but it was Fred's idea, so we went along with it. It's not like the team would locate a fanghead, use a blowgun to shoot him with a tranquilizer dart and put a tag around his neck. Not an endangered species to protect. These are vampires—deadly killers, blood junkies. Sometimes, the crew followed a bloodsucker to see if he could lead the way to others, but the team usually conducted a stake-out that led to a stake-in and a stake-ing… and one less undead in the city.

I scaled the back of the building with a grappling hook. It took three tries to make it stick. The movies always make it look so simple, but a director can edit out all the times it doesn't work. Snagging part of the building is just the beginning of the process. Once the hook is secure, you have to climb the rope. You can't just walk up a wall. There's this thing called gravity that keeps trying to drop you back onto the bone-fracturing pavement. Managed to reach the top without too many rope burns… and only one scraped knee. The roof was a mess. Dry leaves, dirt, old chairs, syringes and animal droppings—this place had it all—and an unlocked door.

Of course, an unlocked door could be a trap but sometimes an unlocked door is just an unlocked door. I went in and headed down a musty corridor.

My body gives me a little heads-up when I'm near vampires. It's nothing like a special glow to the air or a soft angel chorus. It feels like the air is thicker, has more of a texture. This place felt like somebody was trying to stuff a mattress down my throat. I was in the presence of mine enemy… and heard laughter. A voice rose over the sound.

"Yeah, I get that a lot. They've seen too many movies and TV shows. They expect tall, pale and attractive, right?"

There were a few "Yeah" responses.

"Look at me. Short, chubby and balding when I was turned and I'll be that way until the day I'm staked, right?"

Laughter, hoots of approval and some applause greeted his statement. The hallway ended, opening onto a walkway and I looked out into an old factory with fluorescent lighting fixtures—unlit—hanging from the ceiling. Down below sat a candlelit crowd of nearly a hundred happy bloodsuckers. A banner across the end of the room read "COMEDY BITES—Laughter in a Jugular Vein," with a picture of a Happy Face with fangs. On a makeshift stage stood a short, chubby and balding vampire.

"I'm stuck like this, right? There ought to be some way to improve on what nature and life gave us. You buy a cell phone, in a few years you turn it in and get a better one. When do I get an upgrade, huh? When do I get mine?"

Applause and laughter swept the place. The bloodsucker said, "Good night, everybody," and bowed. As for me, the proximity to that many fangers nearly shut down my lungs while the nightwalker left the stage. A thinner vampire strode to the mike/speaker set-up—probably gotten from a defunct karaoke DJ—and said, "Let's hear it for Dominic Segal," and applause filled the Comedy Club of the Living Dead.

The emcee looked out at the audience. He licked his lips.

"All right, friends, there's more performers waiting to come out here at Comedy Bites, where the jokes will slay you."

That line brought out a few boos and hisses.

"Next, we have a sexy little neckbiter who just finished a gig at Club Dead. She has her own style and she's here for you ladies tonight. Put your cold, dead hands together for Belinda Waterhouse."

A petite woman in Jane Austen-style clothing stepped onto the stage amid mild applause from the men, but the females leaned forward, as if they expected something to happen.

24

"How are you doing? Fed on any good cattle, lately?"

That caused sounds of shock and a few hearty laughs.

"Yes. That's right, you heard me, I call them cattle. Humans. People. Cattle. It's the same thing. Admit it. They're lower than we are. We live on them. Come on! Don't you sometimes bite into a neck and expect them to say, 'Moo?'"

The room erupted into cackles and approving hoots. Belinda looked down at a vampire in the front, one surrounded by females, and smirked.

"You men think you're so powerful. You give a girl that look, use your charm and she offers her neck to you. Ladies, you know we don't need glamour. Show a little leg, a little cleavage and he's yours! Who needs magic? Just give 'em a little body language. Sex sells."

The females laughed loudly, the males looked stunned and affronted. What a weapon. The V.I.P. didn't need stakes; we needed joke writers!

"Halvorsen."

Fred's voice in my ear startled me. Blasted communications technology. People you wouldn't want to talk to are right with you, electronically.

"Halvorsen, what are you doing in there? Reading tarot cards? Report in."

He saw me doing it once and he's never let me live it down. Kept my voice low and measured, not wanting to attract attention in a building where a vampire hunter could get his neck ripped out with no trouble at all.

"Team Leader, this is Fast Forward. I have ninety to a hundred bogeys. They're watching a show."

"They're what?"

"It's some kind of comedy club for vampires. An emcee, comedians, a stage and some of the jokes are pretty good."

Fred's voice buzzed in my earpiece.

"I don't care if it's 'America's Got Talent,' Fast Forward. Scope out the access and evaluate attack options. It won't be dark forever."

Had to admit it—he was right. We didn't have a lot of time before the vamps would move out. Hit our targets while they were in one place. Started the recon I should have been doing already: working my way around the perimeter, checking doors and moving down to the lower level. Another comic worked the room. The sound reaching the basement wasn't as clear.

"Does Hollywood ever get us right? Turning into bats, floating with the mist, sparkling—Ohhh, don't get me started on that one—suddenly growing distorted foreheads. Thanks a lot, Joss Whedon. Come on, we're nothing special. It's like having a food allergy, like that celiac thing, a reaction to gluten. Pizza? Can't have it. The garlic gives me gas. Burgers and fries? Not on my diet. Blood? Yeah. That's the ticket."

My lungs felt a little clearer on the lower level (not as many dead bodies moving around). My night-vision equipment picked out a breaker box with some big switches, like the ones in horror movies on a mad scientist's wall, in the "off" position, by the stairs. One was labeled "LIGHTS."

That full feeling in my chest warned me on the stairs. Flipped the safety off my wrist weapons and fired two arrow-stakes in rapid succession. The second one struck heart and the undead bloodbag collapsed into full death with a cheerful sizzle. He wasn't old enough to turn to dust and not new enough to look sunken-cheeked, but he was definitely a melter. His decomposing body fit nicely under the steps.

Back on the upper landing, about time to report in to Team Leader with all the acquired intel. Fred snarled, impatient as usual. It's not like he ran the risks.

"About time, We'll let you know when we're ready to move in. Sit tight."

Sit tight? What's a person supposed to do while hiding from dozens of hemoglobin-happy neck-nippers? I watched the aggressive stand-up routine happening on the stage. He was pointing at a stylish blood-drinker who had his arm around the shoulder of a female.

"Ooh, look at the scary, scary vampire! Oh, come on! Not that long ago, you were working at K-Mart. Does this sound familiar?"

The insult comic leaned into the microphone. The distorted voice rang out.

"Clean-up on aisle seventeen."

The guy stepped back and resumed his verbal assault on the other vamp. "Now, you're Mister I've-Got-Fangs-and-I'm-Cool. Right? And I'm the Tooth Fairy."

The female was laughing and poking the put-down blood-boy, which wasn't the smartest thing to do. It got the attention of the fang-bearing Rickles wannabe.

He said, "Oh, and look at Little Miss Vampire Queen, with your eye makeup that's thicker than stucco. Think you're hot, dontcha? I've seen hotter bods on 'The Walking Dead' and they're room temperature."

The girl didn't think that was funny and started to pout, but the club's Merchant of Venom had moved on to other topics.

"Now, how did zombies get more popular than us? Vampires are becoming yesterday's news. It's zombie this and zombie that! I don't think zombies are all that great. I mean, vampires just have to break the skin and we've got all the hot blood we can drain, but zombies? Think about it. The skull is the hardest bone in the body. To get at a brain, it's like cracking a ten-pound coconut. That's too much work for me. Give me blood anytime."

The crowd cheered his affirmation of their lifestyle. He bowed a few times, waved and exited. The cadaverous host took the mike.

"Now, something special for you, a *new*, f-f-f-fresh talent…"

There was something nasty in the way he said that and in the leering smirk on his face.

"We've been looking for someone like this, now it's your opportunity."

His salacious grin grew wider.

"Here she is—Kim Cooper!"

Pushed onto the stage was…

My jaw dropped. She was young. She was built along friendly lines. She was... pink. She wasn't pale like all the other comics and the audience. She had tone, color and human beauty in a roomful of hemoglobin-swilling freaks.

Kim gazed at the tableau in front of her. A deer caught in the headlights of an eighteen-wheeler looks more aware. She grinned.

"Wow! You guys look great! They told me this gig was different, but this is some of the best cosplay I've ever seen! What neat costumes and the make-up looks, like, really real! Grigor said that you're a terrific audience, that you'd just eat me up."

There was a crackling sound in my ear.

"Fast forward, come in."

"We have a problem, Team Leader, A friendly in the killzone."

Fred asked, "What's she doing there?"

"Getting ready to tell jokes, I think, and get eaten."

"Can you get her out of there?"

"I—I think—" I said, frantically searching my brain for an idea that had a chance of success, and I found one. "Yes, I can. Is the team ready?"

"In place and ready to go."

"Wait for my signal."

"This better work, Halvorsen. Out," Fred said and was silent.

"Yeah, it better," I muttered.

I watched Kim as I headed for the basement. She had a small stack of cards she was checking as she talked.

"What's a vampire's favorite drink?"

She answered herself.

"A Bloody Mary... with real blood."

There were groans, but Kim kept going.

"How does a vampire cross the ocean? On a blood vessel."

A deep voice said, "I didn't," which got more laughs than Kim's joke.

"What's a vampire's favorite fruit? Necktarines."

Her heckler responded.

"Forget the –tarines. Let's just neck."

That went over great with his peers.

I reached the switches and could hear her. Unfortunately.

"Why does nobody like Dracula? He's a real pain in the neck."

"I got your pain in the neck right here!"

The crowd was getting rowdier and the girl didn't have much time left.

I announced, "Team, we go fluorescent in three... two... one... Now!"

I took off the night-vision goggles and flipped the switches to up-positions.

It was a flicker of brightness first, blossoming into day-sharp harshness: fluorescent lighting, illuminating the undead.

It didn't kill them or make them burst into flame—couldn't be that lucky—but the ultra-violet from the overhead fixtures sapped some of their power and energy, giving the Team a fighting chance. The doors burst open and the V.I.P. went to work.

Philips and Reiker had crossbows, shooting bolts into anything with fangs. Wendy did her best Buffy the Vampire Slayer imitation, kicking, stabbing and staking. Fred directed from a safe distance, shouting directions and orders to the fighters, occasionally stopping to pound kill-stakes into any bodies that were still trying to move.

With all the suckerfaces around me, it felt like trying to breathe gelatin as I fought my way toward the stage. With only two of my arrow-stakes left on one arm, who should my next opponent be?

The club emcee, Grigor.

The gaunt throat-jockey pulled out a foot-long knife and said, "Hope it's a good day to die for you, buddy, because I plan to stick around for a while."

I triggered my wrist-launcher, sure of my aim. He snatched the wooden missile out of the air before it hit him. So much for his being in a light-induced, weakened condition. How fast would he be at full strength?

"I've been in this un-life for a long time. I won't go easy, my friend."

He lunged, but he'd slowed enough for me to get out of his knife-reach and close enough to a wooden chair to grab it and swing it against the night-walker. It staggered him, but he didn't go down. He went at me again, so I used the chair as a shield, jabbing and feinting at the sharp-featured creature. I chair-clubbed him and the seat sheared off, leaving me with the back and a broken stile, the back's vertical edge. I tried to fend off my adversary's next slash too late and blood spurted from my left arm.

He seemed mesmerized by the sight. He rushed at me in bloodlust, right into my last arrow-stake and the infernal impresario vaporized into a cloud of bone dust.

I hurried onto the stage, where Kim huddled in a corner, shivering.

"Are you all right?"

"What happened?"

"Those weren't geeks in make-up. They were real vampires. We got here just in time."

She was breathtaking. I couldn't breathe. I couldn't breathe.

I couldn't…

Breathe.

I knew why.

I shoved the stile of the chair-back into her chest. Her mouth opened in pain and I could see the fangs.

"A girl's… got to… try."

The lines deepened in her heavy make-up. When she started to go gooey and drippy, I stood up and backed away.

Fred put a hand on my shoulder.

"You never know, Halvorsen. You never know."

Kim Cooper. Her routine: pretending to be a human in a crowd of vampires.

You know how it is. In comedy, everybody has a gimmick.

The Dragon Detector

Elana Gomel

The call came at 3.40 pm and woke me up. Afternoon is the worst time of day. It's sandwiched between the morning when everything seems fresh and ripe with promise and the evening when darkness gives you a decent pretext for going to bed. In the afternoon the sky is glassy, the sun merciless and you feel passage of wasted time as physically as bleeding.

The call was from Rose, of course, though she used another anonymous number. But who else would be calling me? David only did when there was some loose end of the divorce business to settle and Cassie...

"SFO," said Rose's clipped voice in my ear. "Third terminal."

I savored the burst of adrenaline. Unfortunately I am immune to substance abuse. Alcohol passes through my body like water; pot gives me migraines; the antidepressants that I was prescribed after the divorce had all the efficacy of sugar pills. My brain, with its "unique and precious software" as Rose put it, serves the state's interests well. It does nothing for me.

I drove to the airport in my new SUV. Pale sunshine oozed down my windshield, curdled by the grit in the air. The Vacaville fire-dragon had been bad. Half the town was smoking ruins by the time the dragon collapsed in upon itself, tunneling into a point of nothingness above the charred ground.

It was not my fault, I kept telling myself. Too bad I cannot not get addicted even to self-deception.

The traffic was light, so I got to SFO in record time. They were waiting for me: Rose and two of her interchangeable goons. I could never fix their faces in my memory. They all blended into one generic image like a stock photo: a thick neck, a crewcut and a blank stare. I am not good at face recognition. I am not good at anything, except the one thing that makes me indispensable.

The goons took care of parking and escorted me through the chaos of the airport, parting the crowds like twin avatars of Moses marching through the Red Sea. And if this was not enough to assure me of my importance, Rose Delano, the FBI director herself, was limping by my side.

It turned out to be a new eatery called Farm-something or other and featuring all-organic salads, gluten-free sandwiches and Napa wines. I was glad it was not a luggage carousel. Nothing is worse than standing by the hypnotically floating succession of identical suitcases, peering at their scuffed leather and waiting for the sharp crack of a hatching.

The eatery had been evacuated. I stepped over the yellow tape. Rose moved to follow me, her scrunched-up body in a ridiculously formal black suit hovering like a crow. I shook my head and she moved back. It was not to protect her. If the dragon hatched before I located the egg, a couple of extra yards would not make any difference. At the end of the day, the entire San Francisco International

Airport could be a wilderness of ashes or a swamp overflowing with pungent slime. But I needed to be alone when I was working. Other people were a distraction to me – as David had never failed to point out.

I stopped in the middle of the eatery, taking it all in: the lifeless fluorescent glare; the abandoned plastic plates, overflowing with dying vegetables and dead meat; the xylophone of multicolored sodas in the fridge; the bulging shapes of wine bottles like a row of portly Victorian gentlemen …When I *look*, I need to empty out my mind. I need to be fully present in the moment – not second-guessing myself, not figuring out, not thinking at all – just *looking*. Perhaps that was why I failed, time and again, to train a successor. How could I explain my "method" when there was no method at all?

I could see nothing except for the flotsam of transient lives. Panic welled up in my throat.

I glanced back at Rose. Her reconstructed face was not made for expressing emotions but I knew she was frightened. We were standing near a hand-grenade with a lit fuse.

I squinted at the salad bar under the sloping glass cover. The colors were smudged somehow: the red ripeness of tomatoes clotting into maroon; the cheerful green of arugula deepened into somber sage… It looked strange but then I realized it was because the glass of the case was oily, painted with swirls of fatty deposits. I went back staring at the wine bottles, their uniform darkness promising some secret locked inside, even though I knew it

35

was dangerous to succumb to the obvious symbolism of everyday life.

I heard the tapping of Rose's high-heeled shoe on the floor.

Rose was not born with a curved spine and a shiny plastic mask for a face. The Orlando dragon, one of the first ones to evolve beyond the simplicity of fire- and smoke-drakes, had made her what she was now. There had been so many more since then: water-dragons, to poison rivers and make the Caspian Sea into a giant reservoir of acid; flesh-dragons, to breed swarms of flying leeches that burrowed into the bodies of the victims; slime-dragons, to vomit forth waves of suffocating, greasy foam...

Grease! I sprinted toward the salad bar, ran my hand over the glass and felt it give, stickily, like a liquefying corpse.

"This!" I yelled, pointing to the bar.

The agents moved with a lightning speed and I just managed to flop down and roll out of the way as a hailstorm of bullets shattered the case. The noise was deafening but still could not drown the screams in the terminal. I wondered how many people would be prevented by PTSD from ever entering an airport again. Carbon taxes and pandemics had failed to stem the flow of air traffic; perhaps dragons would. I assumed that this was the terrorists' calculus.

The rattle of bullets died down and I risked raising my head. The pseudo-farm looked like it was growing broken glass instead of produce. Streams of wine and rivulets of soda mingled in a complicated beverage delta on the floor. My gaze was instantly drawn to a smashed tray that used to hold quinoa salad and I felt the tension drain out of my body.

'The tray was swollen and puffy. The scattered grains of quinoa, inflated to the size of a ball bearing, quivered, jelly-like. And from a pile of chopped vegetables, a single curved talon, as big as my hand, stuck out.

I was right. That had been the dragon egg.

I waited for Cassie to call until I could plausibly lie to myself that it was too late and she was already in bed. Of course, I knew she was probably chatting with her girlfriends on the phone. David never insisted on reasonable hours. Nevertheless, I was a bad mother. He was a stay-at-home dad, a perfect parent. The fact that it was my money that made it possible for him to go freelance, while having full custody, was irrelevant.

I could call or text Cassie myself...to have my call rejected and my text go unanswered. And then tomorrow there would be a brief impersonal response and behind it I could hear David's mildly reproachful voice, saying, "Cas, she is your mum!" and Cassie's resentful grunt. So I went to bed. Not to sleep – I would doze off after midnight if I was lucky – but to feel safe and protected in my cocoon. I had piled up old books on the other side of the bed where David used to sleep. I turned on the TV. Surrounded by books and fragrant candles, I could cope with the state of the world. Sometimes I thought it would be nice to have a pet but I was allergic to cats. As for dogs... one of the first eggs I had discovered was in a sweet little Chihuahua.

The discovery of a dragon egg at SFO was not top of the newscast. Unsurprising, considering what was. A dragon had hatched in the Old City of Basel in Switzerland. The newsfeed showed shell-shocked people staring pleadingly into the camera as if expecting to see the faces of their lost loved ones on the other side of the screen. A giant Catherine wheel was sagging over the demolished cathedral; a 700-year-old bridge was reduced to a path of rubble across the shallow Rhine. It had been a stone drake, a heavy lumbering beast, shedding rocks as it worked its way through the Marketplatz crowds.

I turned the TV off and lay on my back, staring at the ceiling dappled with writhing shadows from the candles. The sales of home candles and decorative lights had gone down because people mistakenly associated them with fire-drakes. In fact, dragon eggs could be placed in any object and there was no apparent connection between the incubator and the type of dragon that hatched from it. You played Russian roulette when you bought a loaf of bread, a grandfather clock, or a pet rabbit.

But not me. A hatched dragon could not be killed; it simply collapsed into nothingness when its brief lifetime had run its course. But before the hatching, the egg could be destroyed. And I was the only one who could see an egg inside its everyday disguise.

A gust of wind rattled the windowpane. I knew I was under constant surveillance, which did not bother me. Pathetically, it provided a sense of

38

company. After the divorce, I found out all my friends had been David's. My parents were dead. I was a pathological loner and it made Rose's job much easier. She did not have to worry about a visitor planting an egg in my dishwasher or sofa. A terrorist had to be on the scene physically to do whatever they did to turn an everyday object into a monster incubator.

Nobody knew what it was. Rose would undoubtedly administer any kind of torture to a terrorist to find out the secret of sowing dragon eggs, the Geneva Convention be damned. But no terrorist had ever been captured alive. All had eggs nesting in their bodies and attempting to arrest them would merely loose yet another nasty indestructible beast.

The White House and most of Washington DC had closed to all visitors. But you cannot fence in airports, malls or streets. Or National Parks. Or a random stretch of public land. The last wood dragon that hatched in the Bay Area turned a neighborhood's favorite hiking trail into a palisade of sharpened sticks where joggers and dog-walkers hung, impaled.

The FBI received tips, of course; this was how Rose had known about SFO. But she never told me about her sources and my timid attempts at asking questions were met with silence. I was just a useful tool. A human-shaped dragon detector.

Cassie called me when I was in the supermarket. When I saw my daughter's face on the screen, I dropped a package of frozen peas onto the floor and lunged toward a quiet corner.

"Hi, Mum!" That word sat awkwardly on her lips whose shape had changed since the last time I saw her. They were fuller and rosier.

Cassie is beautiful. I am not. But there has never been any resentment on my side. Maybe it is because I do not think of myself as a woman. I am a little sexless scarecrow hiding in the corner. I am a weird geek with pale eyes and thin mousy hair. I am Ash.

Cassie takes after her father, whose courtship of me was one of those inexplicable miracles that only come once in a lifetime. I was lucky; I had two of them.

"Hi, darling!" I said, too chirpily. "How are you? How's school?"

Her face clouded over and I berated myself. Here I was, squandering this rare and precious opportunity by nagging!

"School's OK," she said vaguely. "Hey, Mum, can we meet today?"

At first I thought I had misheard. Initially Cassie was to spend every second weekend with me but after a year of my being constantly called away, David had convinced me that Cassie was better off without being jerked between two homes. "She needs stability in her life," he had said in that soothing voice whose magic did not fade even after the divorce. "It's a vulnerable age and she's already been through so much..." He didn't need to finish that sentence. I agreed.

40

Since then I only talked to Cassie when David, always conscientious, urged her to phone me. I was screwing up my courage to negotiate an overnight stay at Thanksgiving but it was two months away. And here she was, asking me for a meeting!

"Of course, darling!" I said, hoping she could not hear the choking in my voice. "Anytime."

I barely recognized my daughter.

Not because she had grown – that was expected. Not because she was even more beautiful than before – I had seen it even through the smudged glass of my phone. But because there was now an edge to this beauty, a strange febrile glow. She seemed to leave a trail of sparks as she walked into Peet's. Heads turned.

I felt as if our roles had suddenly switched as if I was an awkward and insecure teenager, about to be rebuked by a stern parent.

I asked if she wanted a Coke.

"Water," she said.

She drank slowly while I raked my brain trying to guess what she could possibly want from me that she could not get from her father. Finally I hit on one plausible explanation: that she was pregnant. I was ashamed to realize that it cheered me up; at least, she would need me for something.

But when Cassie finally spoke, it had nothing to do with a visit to Planned Parenthood.

"Mum, can you teach somebody else to become a dragon detector?"

I choked on my stewed tea.

"You know I can't talk about it!"

41

My daughter's luminous green eyes she had not inherited from me did not leave my face and my resolve melted away.

"No," I said truthfully. "I can't teach anybody. I don't think it can be taught."

"So what is it?"

"It's… it's like an inborn talent. Hereditary."

And then I saw it.

"No!" I yelled so loudly that a couple of patrons turned their heads in my direction. "No," I repeated, lowering my voice to an agitated hiss. "Don't even think about it! You don't have it!"

"How do you know?"

"Because… because…" I cast around, feeling lost because *how* did I know it? "Because you're not like me. We're different."

"But I'm your daughter!"

"Yes," I said. "You're my daughter. And I'd know if you had my… my talent. But I'm pretty sure you don't. I knew I had it since I was six. You're sixteen."

"But there were no dragons when you were six, were there?"

"No," I said, "there were no dragons. The Children of Gaia got active when you were about ten. But I knew I had a special sight. I could find lost objects and see into locked safe-boxes, that kind of things. My parents suspected I would become a stage magician and were horrified."

That elicited a wan smile from her.

I was about to launch into the safe waters of childhood recollections when Cassie, once again, steered our conversation in an unexpected direction:

"What did you think when it started? The Children of Gaia?"

I shrugged.

"What could I think? The same as any rational person on the planet: they're crazy and evil."

"Even though they're saying they try to prevent a catastrophe?"

"That's what all terrorists say. Whatever they are fighting against is the greatest evil… blah-blah. And then they kill a bunch of innocent people. Even if they manage to achieve their goal, they'll turn out to be worse than whoever or whatever they are trying to overthrow."

"How can anything be worse than the extinction of life on Earth?"

I blinked. Did my daughter really come to meet me in order to discuss politics? I had steeled myself for *the* question that had blighted our relationship. I had weighed and discarded various answers:

I did not really leave you…

It was Dad's decision too, not mine alone.

We were trying to do what was best for you.

Anything but confessing the humiliating truth: that when David told me he did not love me anymore I went to pieces. I could not pull myself together enough to care for my daughter. And when I finally crawled out from under the pall of depression, it was too late: the divorce agreement had been signed and Cassie, sullen and dry-eyed, moved into her dad's new house.

But this? Was she baiting me? When I was her age, radical ecology had been a thing and hip teenagers talked about "curing the planet from the

43

disease of humanity." But since the dragon attacks started, the public opinion had undergone a shift. To talk about climate change was to side with the dragon sowers, and nobody wanted to be suspected as a sympathizer.

"That's what their manifestoes say," I said. "Who knows if they are for real? No terrorist has even been apprehended, so maybe it's a bunch of crap. Maybe they are just having fun killing people."

"Fun? Sacrificing themselves in the process?"

This finally got my goat.

"Fanatics don't value their own lives because they don't value other people's lives," I said, more sharply than I intended. "And if I were you, Cassie, I would give it a rest. After Basel, people won't appreciate theoretical debates about the ethics of mass murder!"

I expected an angry retort but she just stared into her empty glass. Her phone pinged; she glanced at it and rose to her feet.

"Got to go."

I got up too, longing to hug her but afraid of rejection. And then another miracle happened: she lunged forward and put her arms around me.

"It was good to see you, Mum," she mumbled into my sweater.

"It was good to see you too, sweetie," I managed to whisper. "Maybe we can do it again soon."

Cassie stepped back and I saw a tear crawl down her cheek.

"Maybe," she said and was out of the coffee-shop before I could find anything else to say. But it did not matter. I walked on clouds as I went back to my car.

My daughter cried because she was parting from me!

The rest of the day went by in a happy glow. I fantasized about mending the fences with Cassie, having her come over, stay overnight, perhaps eventually moving in with me...

Rose called just before bedtime. Her glistening mask of a face filled the screen. The Orlando dragon had spat jets of organic acid that literally melted the flesh off her bones.

"Ashley," she said and fell silent. I waited, resentful that she was intruding on my bliss but also feeling the first stirrings of excitement.

"There has been a... tip."

"Where?" Rose's unwonted hesitation seemed to indicate that my next assignment involved long-distance flying. She knew I hated planes.

"It's about you."

"Me?"

"We received information there may be an assassination attempt."

It took a moment for this to sink in.

"I'm the target?"

"Yes."

The phone almost slipped out of my sweat-slicked hand.

"What are you going to do?"

"There are already agents around your house, so don't worry, nobody can get in. But I think it's not enough. You're unique. Irreplaceable. We need to move you to a safe location."

I groaned, looking at the familiar mess of my bedroom and feeling like a snail about to be yanked out of her shell.

"Where?"

"I'd rather not say. The line is encrypted but still… Anyway, you have ten minutes to pack."

My protests sounded unconvincing even to myself and Rose paid them no attention. With a sigh, I walked to the bathroom to select the necessary toiletries. I clicked on the light and met my own eyes in the mirror.

Pale writhing flames wormed their way through the tunnels of my pupils.

I caught myself on the edge of the sink, pressing my face into the glass, telling myself it was an illusion, or an incipient migraine, or a brain tumor. But I knew. I was the dragon detector. The one and only. I saw hatching dragons as they grew in wood, stone, or flesh.

A dragon was growing in me. Somebody had planted an egg in my body. And there was no mystery about who it had been.

I stumbled back to the bedroom. The strange thing was that there were no strange sensations. I'd seen the dragon inside myself but I'd not felt it yet. Not as I had felt my daughter growing inside me, announcing her eventual arrival with morning sickness, bloat and baby kicks. My daughter, a sweet little monster feeding on my blood.

Cassie had been recruited by the terrorists. Did she truly believe that killing her mother was the way to save Mother Earth? Was she a sociopath? A resentful little bitch? Was she trying to pay me back for abandoning her?

What did I know about her? What do parents know about their children?

I pulled the drawer of my bedside table and there it was, a sleek little gun Rose had given me and insisted I learn how to use.

Once a dragon egg is implanted in a living body, it has to hatch unless the body is destroyed. There is no way to cut it out. But I still had some time before a beast clawed its way out of me, unfurled it leathery wings or stretched its scaly appendages and rained fire, or spat acid, or trampled cities. Would some remnant of myself survive in the monster? Would I delight in making others suffer as I suffered?

I still had enough time to pick up my phone and call Rose. Enough to tell her David's address.

No terrorist had ever been apprehended but even one arrest could start unraveling the whole organization of the Children of Gaia. If they came upon her suddenly, put her under sedation... The terrorists must have some way to delay or even neutralize the hatching of a dragon egg. After all, in previous attempts to capture a suspect alive, they would hatch their egg instantly, while having gone through months and maybe years with it lying dormant in their bodies.

Perhaps Cassie knew the secret. Perhaps there was still hope for me.

But none for Cassie. She would be arrested, interrogated and executed. The new Defense of Humanity Act gave extraordinary powers to the security services.

Cassie. A sower of dragons. A terrorist. A would-be matricide.

My daughter.

I lifted the gun and clicked the safety off.

There is only one way to kill a dragon. Destroy its egg.

I pressed the muzzle to my forehead.

Empty Nest

Sarah Townend

Folded neatly, that's how she left the pile of freshly laundered and pressed towels in each room. Every nook and cranny and each bare shelf and untouched toy in the children's rooms dusted every day, despite the cribs now resting, unused. The made-up beds lay as cold and quiet as the expectant, refrigerated body lockers down at the dead house. One day they would return. She was certain that one day they'd need her again.

A fortnight ago, she'd lost her eldest son, Freddie. He hadn't so much as looked back, merely cornered his head for a final goodbye as she'd waved him off in the death trap he'd toiled all summer to buy. Music had blasted out from his car—a most unwanted farewell gift to her ears—and he'd fled the nest for university some hundred and fifty miles south. Jennifer, the daughter with the red hair, had departed five months earlier, again with her first love, a factory worker of some kind, to the coast. Never called her mother.

Her husband, rest his soul, had been gone six years to the day now too. The children, which they were until ever so recently, had encouraged her to try and pack away his belongings. She had of course ignored them, her opinion on the matter being the only one of any value. His books on chess, billiards and all the other sports he had been so absorbed by screamed at her from the shelf. Yet untouched they rested, gathering dust like a grey settling of snow, like the frosting that had appeared at her temples. The children had taken no interest in the games, but she couldn't take them down—she couldn't remove them because even though he was long dead, deep in the ground, a luncheon for snaking worms, his belongings dotted around the house made her feel like someone other than her own sagging figure was still present; the lifeless items of paper, wood, metal and glass made her feel a little less alone.

In defiance of her spiralling solitude, she had brought in his fishing rods and clutter and other ghosts from the garage, displaying them on the sideboard in the living room, perhaps hopeful that his possessions would encourage him up and back from the plot at the bone yard. She'd settle for anyone's company in her prison-cage life, even the husband with whom her words had run dry with decades ago.

Her husband had been a support for the family home, paid the bills, ate her food with gratitude. He had loved her deeply despite knowing his love was travelling aboard a one way ticket. He'd propped them all up, especially her, when she'd had low moments, when nothing could quell the heat from the angry furnace that burnt inside her, or plug up the tears that would rain from her eyes each month, each cycle. She had liked the man in her own way, although love was a word of higher value, a one-off payment that he knew she had already spent elsewhere.

No-one had been there to mop up her tears since he had departed; her children were heartless at best. The Change that followed the loss had triggered a cacophony of emotions that even half quart of gin could not suffocate of an evening. No amount of fanning or air conditioning could counter the flushes either. She'd taken to stripping off naked in the night, around two or three, feeling lost, shipwrecked on the surface of the sun, dripping with cling-wrapped limbs coated in her own perspiration and gliding about the house, sticky, searching for something to cool her down and something more than gin to bring her sleep.

Whilst cleaning, a hobby she partook in on her better days to fill her hours, a hobby that played out quite synergistically alongside the hoarding of Robert's old belongings, she found an old photograph album. It poured out faded, dull memories—images of another time—from way before she had met her husband. She leafed through the black and white photographs mounted on fragile sheets, each picture triggering little within. Perhaps time and the loss of the hormones that once made her shine had dulled her senses, numbed her essence. Her well of emotion had perhaps dried like every other part of her papery, parched shell; until she reached the end of the album.

And there it was, popping out at her, jumping out and off the page, striking her heart—a cue ball potting a red on a break—bringing a flurry of warmth to her core. The hag felt a flush to her joints more so than any of the moments the Change had delivered so far. There it was, exhumed from wherever her subconscious had chosen to bury it, smothered by the tiredness of early motherhood and the demands of running the family home and sustaining a mundane marriage... there it was: her happy memory.

Michael Baker had been her high school sweetheart, her one true love. He had been the sun to her moon, the steak knife to her fork and they had been together, although only for a turn of a season. With him, she had felt invincible. Never since had she felt a passion so strong or the obsessive need to be touched, felt and held—not even the gift she'd been informed each of her children would bring had matched the sensation. In the snapshot that felt her fingertips brushing a-top, she and Michael Baker stood, embraced like knotted vines, her eyes only on him and his eyes only on her. Her palm travelled to her chest and rested against her heart, guarding it, uncertain whether the chest-plummet she was feeling could be caught as joy or pain. He had sold her the world, given her the moon on a stick, but of course as her parents had hinted, it had all been puppy love.

Over the summer before they had all parted to go to college, to carve their own paths through life, she had caught him kissing another in the spot where they too had taken their first kiss. The sight of his lips, his hands on another had cracked her heart in two that day, it had split like a dropped melon on a stone floor, a mirror shattered yielding a lifetime of bad luck. She had slowly tried to patch the pieces back together and to make some kind of mosaic from the thousand shards scattered by his deed, but everything had felt surreal since, distorted, fractured and untrue.

She peeled out the single photograph, held it tightly to her heart and carried it and her face now full of tears into her bedroom. Here she propped up the cherished photo in front of the long-ignored bedside filigree frame, back-seating a snap from her wedding day—her and her late husband, both holding a knife, cutting the cake.

Bitter tears rolled hellward, down her cheek as she threw herself back onto her bed at three in the afternoon and there she remained a full half-spin, until three in the morning, falling down a shaft of misery and nostalgia, drowning in tears merged with the sweat the night brought her, with no soul there to pull her out.

It was pitch black when she woke, all stars were asleep and even the crescent-sliver of moon must have been taking a timely blink from its eternal stretch of velvet sky. The cherished photo of her and her high school lover had slipped down, dragged perhaps into her well of misery, lost at sea, somewhere in the bed amongst the drenching waves of sheets. Her framed wedding photo stood proud, erect, glaring at her victoriously from its filigree frame. If you were to look closely enough at her face captured in the wedding snap, on her Special Day, you'd see she was indeed smiling despite the matrimony being rather a facade. You'd see a red slash of lips across her pale, smooth face—quite a vision before time reaped her beauty—and the corners of her lips were pinned up, nailed almost to her apple cheeks, but her eyes were flat, as if she wasn't fully there.

She fumbled in the bed in search of the other photo, of her and Michael Baker that she'd bawled at and stared at until she'd eventually capsized and dropped off into a hurricane of horizontal insensibility, but it was to no avail; gone. Emptiness smacked her and lifted her like a hand from the heavens, depositing her back into sweet hell. At least she could still see her young lover's face when she closed her eyes. Her heart bled out, pain flooded her arteries, her eyes ran dry—she had no tears left to cry.

But she still had the knife from her wedding.

***

Under the devilish slice of a honeydew crescent moon now open and staring again, she slumped out of bed, crouched on the floor amongst many an old thing and pulled out the suitcase in which her wedding dress was stored. She flipped open the metal clasps of the trunk and carefully drew out the over-engineered garment. Thirty years and the fabric itself had not perished even slightly, it was still as cream as the day she had worn it all those years ago, as milky-white as the parts of her body untouched by the sun and also now, due to its storage, as crumpled and folded as her own badly-aged skin-suit. But it was not the dress she was after.

Several more photographs rested underneath the gown and a blue garter made of silk, not borrowed but new and now also old and a wooden spoon a great aunt had gifted her for one

54

superstitious reason or another. In a zipped compartment at the bottom of the case was an item shrouded in newspaper from the sixties—tatty, yellowed and pressed tightly around the wedding piece.

A smile slit across her face, breaking through the dried rivulets set where tears had fallen before sleep had come. She unwrapped the baroque-handled blade from its old home and held it in her older hands. It was the same blade she had used to cut up her wedding cake into a hundred or so small slices and it had cut through the first piece as sharply and keenly as the last all those years ago. Large and long and still as sharp as a throat-razor. She held it up in the air. She noted that it had tarnished slightly as she peered into it—drunk on tiredness, drunk on the Change, inquisitive as to what she might see, searching perhaps for a vision, a prophetic mirage—but it was still bright enough to return only her disappointing reflection. Who was this careworn witch looking back? Was this why Michael Baker, her first love, her only true love, the one she had loved perhaps more than life itself, had left her for another?

***

He'd married her friend—her enemy. They were still together as far as she knew; back down in the backwaters, the boondocks of Claretville. Although the old school gossip was thin on the ground, lapsing and fading like her once glossy head of hair as people moved away by Ford or by hearse, she most likely would have heard if they had of parted.

Her sadness swung to rage, a weathercock on a windy day, as she tried to block out the face of the friend who had stolen her Love all those years ago. She pulled on clothes and shoes with no thought of appearance and, wrapping the blade back up in its newspaper casing, she placed the bundle into her handbag. With her keys in her hand, she stormed out to her car, something strong whipped up inside.

Out in the car, hands on wheel ten-to-two, on a night cold enough to see her own breath, she thought of his. She could still remember how Michael's breath had smelt of coffee and caramel, sweet, distinctive. She remembered how she loved to kiss him in the evening, or after he'd come off the rugby pitch when his scent, the tang of his lips, would taste like a concentrated version of himself. She reached into the glove box and pulled out a red lipstick, *Ruby Kiss*, that, like herself, hadn't been handled for years. She smeared it over her dry lips without so much as a glance in the rear-view mirror, she circled her mouth thrice to be sure; her face, her lips akin now to a bleeding womb, primed with or for determination fuelled by loss. She had never enjoyed kissing her husband and was thankful once the children arrived, thus qualifying exhaustion as an excuse to avoid his intimacy. After a while, her husband had simply stopped trying.

But Michael, oh. She momentarily closed her eyes, returning her hands to the wheel.

He will be mine again.

She needed to fight for her man—the man she wanted. She needed to claim the prize she deserved for all the sufferance she had endured, night after night in her family home with two children who ignored her and a husband she had grown through slow time only to like.

How dare that bitch steal her lover! That is not what friends do. She had not spoken to the thief, Carmine Bridewell, since the day she caught them kissing, although she had screamed the trollop's name into the wind on many a full moon. And now, just thinking her wretched name, mouthing the godforsaken name in angry silence to the space inside of the car felt abrasive to her lips.

She drove into the night, one hand on the wheel and the other in and out of her bag, restless hands, checking the blade was still there whilst the stars turned in the sky and the moon judged down.

She pulled up and flicked off her lights, then sat in the car outside the house of her former lover, where he lived with Carmine, the piece of work he had left her for. The sun broke the horizon, shouting out soundless vermillion and rust all the way and she watched as curtains were drawn open in the house of her Love.

Carmine Bridewell, now Baker, was there, at each window, moving from room to room with haste, spreading open each set of floral drapes, wiping away condensation with a cloth, frowning at the break of day and all that lay ahead.

She watched from her car, concealed by a bush as she contemplated where she'd strike the whore first when she answered the front door. Where would the silvery blade last used to cleave slices of sponge from a three-tier cake enter this stupid, life-robbing slut's body? She bit her lip thinking about the crimson fluid that would leak from her, spurt out from her chest and her thigh and her stomach. She would then scarper, lay low for weeks, a month maybe tops, time enough for a funeral, a wake to come and go before claiming back the man she loved. She would get her happy-ever-after.

The door was closed behind her gently so as not to awaken neighbours. She crept closer to the house; up the path marked out by well-pruned rose bushes, thorn-sharp, blood-red, to the front door of Love's cottage. Her blade lay cold and hard, concealed by a flap of cardigan as she knocked three times on the door.

Through the door she heard a man's voice, it was his voice for sure—her Love—but it boomed and yelled and did not bring joy to her ears like the sweet whispers of nothing she remembered from all those years ago. This voice made her quiver in her boots, it made her heart shudder, beat double pace.

"Who the fucking heck is that, knocking on our door at six o'clock in the morning, woman?" He paused only for breath, to add more venom to his spit. "You answer it, you fucking whore of a woman. You cunt. Then fetch me my fucking breakfast. And if you dare burn my bacon again, you'll speak to my fists."

A thump followed, audible enough to shake birds from the tree-top, then silence, then footsteps.

The lady ran with a capricious, sudden change of heart, back up the path, back up to and around the bush that shielded her car, back into her driving seat. There she sat; a thousand bats of dusk or dawn crashing into her rib cage as her heart pumped them out from the bell tower she had become. In a cold state of dread, hunched low with one eye squinted open and the other firmly closed, she sat as still as rigor mortis, afraid of seeing the state of a beast of a man he'd become and, despite her tool, fearful for her own safety. There she sat, watching, paralysed by fear, her thought clouded with shock.

Carmine opened the door. The same Carmine from her school days, the very same friend who stole her man, but this Carmine had not travelled well with time. Her hair, mostly grey, was swept up into a tangled bun and her eyes were both bruised black. On the top of her bare, sagged arms were more bruises, yellowing but large, the shape of a man's thumb print and once open wounds too from where a ring or belt or both may have struck. A scar ran down her left cheek that looked like it had received stitches, a strip of train track from eye to jaw and as Carmine looked around, searching for whoever had knocked, the lady in the car could see that Carmine's eyes were already dead.

No-one was there. She shut the door and scuttled off to fetch her husband breakfast, like the dutiful wife she was; the enslaved, downtrodden wench she had become.

The lady watching from the car masked by bushes sobbed and waited for minutes in which a lifetime of pain and misery, not her own, flashed through her mind. She clutched her handbag and its contents up to her chest. Then, when she could hear no more shouting or thumping or dishes emptied of crisp bacon becoming smashed, she took her chance and ran back up the garden path. She left a gift wrapped in newspaper by a flower pot with 'For Carmine' scribbled in marker pen on its top, before rushing back to her car and driving away, top speed, like she had some place else she needed to be.

And she did. And she didn't.

She drove home.

For now, her home felt like a place of freedom, a place of no responsibility. It may have been an empty nest but it was her nest and it was a nest from which she could now leave, either as a dropped egg or a winged bird. It was a nest from which she was now free.

After a lengthy bath to cleanse her skin of panic, she'd have blue steak for breakfast. Why not? Who could tell her otherwise—

Middle-age was a dish best served alone.

Deadly Masquerade

Chris Marchant

I look again at the old woman, "Why do I need a mask?"

"I can feel the pull, you must follow the call," she says.

"What call? I hear nothing," I look around, although the street is crowded, it's fairly quiet.

She laughs, "It's a call of the spirit, not of the ears. Here, you will need the mask, it's a time when the inner spirit must lead and the outer self must be hidden."

"I have no time for this nonsense," I push the mask away again.

"You will learn the truth of who and what you are tonight." She rams the mask into my hands and turns. "Follow the music, just follow the music."

Her voice gets fainter and she's gone. I examine the mask in my hands. It's of a large cat, designed to cover the upper part of the face, sitting on top of the head. The face is silver, with white hair covering the rest of the head. The people passing see the mask and shrink away as if afraid of it. She said, 'follow the music', but there is no music. I put the mask on and there it is, faint, but there in the distance. The beat is infectious, the need to dance overpowering. I consider removing the mask, but curiosity takes over, I need to know more. The people I approach move aside, some of them cower away, others look at me with contempt. This worries me, but is drowned out by the call, the need. I move faster, the walk becomes a run as the music gets louder. Then as I pass through a gateway, the music stops. The courtyard is empty and my footsteps echo. The silence is deafening. Now my mind starts working again, why am I here? What am I doing? I start raising my hands to remove the mask, but then very quietly, a new melody starts and the spell tightens around me again, drawing me further in. There are glimpses of others, all masked, seen out of the corners of my eyes. They are hovering, watching, almost a dancelike motion surrounding the edges. The music leads, I pass through room after room with my attentive audience following. The draw is irresistible, uncontrollable, I want to remove the mask, but my hands won't obey me. It must be the mask; it has to be some kind of spell. Why me?

The music gets louder and finally my feet stop. The room is huge and glittering with gold. It slowly fills with the people who followed me, all masked. They take up places surrounding the floor, all eyes on me. Directly in front is a large chair, like a throne, empty. The music in my head dies away and I am free to move again, I immediately look behind me, but those doors are closed and the audience fills all the sides. The only gaps are those either side of the throne. The room is unnaturally quiet, not a whisper disturbs the silence, so the sudden sound of a door opening cuts through the air like a gunshot. The footsteps echo as they approach. A woman walks into view, coming from behind the throne. She is tall, with jet black hair and very pale luminous skin, with the confidence of maturity. She wears a long silver dress and a cat shaped headdress, the match to my mask. She walks up and inspects me, going around me a few times.

"Passable," she says.

I try to speak, but I'm frozen. She stands in front of me, raises her hand and the music starts again.

"Shall we dance?"

The paralysis lifts and I take her hand, I'm not much of a dancer, but somehow my body knows the steps. We twirl, dip, spin; covering the floor. My mind is totally focussed on the dance; I'm oblivious to everything else. We slow down and that's when I realise that we are the only two dancing, I start to say something, but she shushes me, placing a finger on my lips. The music changes and I also know this dance, somehow. Many dances later, we stop and she leads me to the throne. I am surprised, surely it's her throne, but she insists and so I sit. A large wave of exhaustion suddenly hits me and I slump. She snaps her fingers and a glass with a golden drink in it appears at my hand, carried by a person in a snake mask. She takes it and gives it to me. I drink and then I notice my hands, they've changed, the skin is wrinkly and saggy and they have brown spots. I stare at them and then reach up to my face, but she stops me, running her hand down my cheek.

"It will be fine, just relax."

I look at her, she's got younger; she looks at the peak of youth. When I first saw her she was in the full bloom of maturity. Dread fills me, she's stealing my life. I have to get out of here before it's too late, while I still have life left. I try to stand, but my legs aren't working. She laughs as everything goes black.

IL MIGLIORE DEL MONDO

Alaric Cabiling

You are trapped in a deluge of nights and lie awake in the darkness. You keep staring at the ceiling fan only to watch any movement.

You expect the fan to fall at any instant, decapitating you, blood spattering on your sheets, walls, your soft and white down covers perfect for lovemaking.

For five more nights, you would be sleep-deprived. You walk in the streets like a nomad robbed of his dreams. You gaze through pitch-black windows, seemingly window-peeping. You tread cobblestone walkways, echoing the sound of your footsteps.

The next day, you lie asleep in the midday heat. Naked and innocent in the sheets, you turn in your sleep restlessly, tossing and turning as you feel Death's cold breath graze the hairs on the back of your neck.

Within a minute, you wake up screaming. Sweat trickling down your midsection, the midday sun perforating the gaps in the shades, you realize you've slept but little. Black patches under your eyes resemble deep bruises. Black coffee drips from a spout in the coffee machine. The sound does little to rouse you. The coffee does not rouse you, despite drinking enough.

You take a shower and dress up for another night of listless wandering. The streets are alive at midnight. People dancing, cooking seafood on the grill, street artists painting portraits in pitch-black darkness, you carouse the metropolis like a man howling in the depths of his emptiness.

A child goes up to you, braves the widespread fear you've driven in the hearts of locals like a stake in a vampire's heart. He reaches out his outstretched palm.

"Irse," you tell him. "Ahora... now!"

The boy smiles unexpectedly then runs away. You wanted a son once. Once, when your wife was living.

You think that only you feel that emptiness. Everywhere, locals here in Santo Domingo, Dominican Republic smile and nod amid a fiesta. Despite poverty, happy locals dance in the height of Mal di Luna—the term the natives use for moon sickness. You call it insomnia, but only you are miserable in the wake of sleeplessness.

At the height of your powers, you are an artist. You do more than draw portraits. You do more than paint beaches. You paint Death in the manner of Poe's Oval Portrait tale: Death in rigor mortis—the hardening of facial muscles, frozen in time to speak eternal loneliness. With faces etched on canvas consisting of an antinomy of colors and dark shades, the robbed heads of patriarchs taken from various family crypts would fetch a ransom few living patriarchs ever could. Your paintings sell well, though, and you've become famous.

But now, midnight passes and you are only too glad to spend late nights amongst primitive locals and savants without painting them. You speak to them in their native tongue—a trick you learned from a woman. The locals are friendly with tourists and you are no exception.

It is midnight and the beaches are empty, save for skinny-dipping locals. Midnight cloaks your rugged features: the gaunt cheeks and blemished, puckered skin, the long face and stark chin, the black patches underneath hardened eyes, the scraggly hair tucked messily behind the small ears.

You were married once but are now alone. You are widowed and your heart bleeds for its other half. You remember her beauty, her kindness, the tenderness of her touch. Everywhere, in crime-ridden Santo Domingo, where streets at night can be lawless and especially dangerous to tourists, the shadows remind you of her absence, her brutal murder at the hands of a demented, perverted local.

You are the unhappy American tourist whom locals know by the name Il Migliore del Mondo—the best in the world—in reference to your work as an artist.

You paint the portraits of putrescent heads.

***

You see, locals fear your presence, but they are driven mad by the chilling realism, the purgatorial afterglow of your portraits. Art that is alive is alive only in Death and only in that Death—that beauty—will locals respect Death as much as life.

Death is no longer a paradigm of the flesh, it is etched in skin, muscle and bone. It manifests in your oil paint and charcoal. It makes itself evident in your blood, sweat and tears. It is a thing of gold.

It is a living harness. It is Death in duress. It is the suspension of decay, the transition between life and disintegration.

You will always be known to them this way.

When you attend social functions, you are dressed for a day with the dead—black—like Death Incumbent. Santa Muerte, your inspiration, would be proud. The socialites fear you, renounce you only in secret. You are like the Red Death coming to the masque to reap the souls of the affluent.

The poor are not immune to your charms. Like a dentist who extracts teeth from the mob's victims, they show indifference while you pass them on broken side streets, fearing you like you are God himself.

Il Migliore del Mondo, guns may come, but your shadow bleeds into the night. Always the police hear about you, but they never come. They never come asking questions, for they already know the answers. They never want the same plight to fall upon their loved ones, their relations—for your charcoal and paints to transpose their souls from harsh realms to even harsher ones—nebulas of ash, bone niter and darkness. They leave you to rot in society's fringes. Yet, in their midst, you are easily a predator amongst prey, a hunter...but never hunted.

When that well-spring of opportunities suits them, even men in the mob—criminals who prey on women and children on the streets—send you charms to entice you, but you refute them. You want nothing of their wares and their methods of making a living from victims.

When they send a woman to your doorstep, they have her go alone. She is confident like any seductress and killer. Like a lioness that leads her pack, she is certain of her skill. You find insult in her attempt at subjugation—she and the lot of them—attempting to usurp your place in the food chain. Else, bend you to their will.

In the background, a trio of musicians plays percussion music. The sounds made from steel drums, steel pans and bongo drums are festive. The woman walks into your promenade, intent on conquering you the way a huntress prematurely kisses her trophy.

You let her in, then taste her. You are not impressed. You smell her perfume. You lavish her set of pearls, her diamond necklace. You raise a tender hand to her cheek. She smiles, underestimates you, reaches for the dagger in her shoal, closes her eyes as if to kiss you warmly, takes your finger inside her, teases you.

She says one thing before she attempts to slay you. "Que pasa si me enamoro de ti?"

What happens if I fall for you?

You aren't convinced. She grasps her dagger. She is ready to kill you. She kisses you but dies as you taste her lips.

***

Blood on your hands, blood on your lips, you stare at the burning moon like a wolf fresh from a kill.

The woman's body at your feet, red dress soaked in crimson, you hold her decapitated head in your hand. Tubular fibers of meat hang from the primitive cut along her neck.

You plan to paint her. You take her head inside. The members of the string quartet hurry out of the promenade after seeing the blood, the headless body. Their job is done. Yours is just beginning.

At home you climb the winding staircase to your studio. The chandelier lights your path; a glint in the eye of the bounty hunter's head in your hand catches the large antique mirror in your dayroom.

Inside your studio, you toss the head to the foot of the trunk. It rolls down the floor and stops there, thudding against the trunk's wooden facade. An eyeball drops out and blood streams out of an ear canal. You don't mind the trail of blood on the floor as you cross the room barefoot.

You take your easel from the closet and take your paint brushes from the trunk. Then, you place the head on a mantle above a pillar. Like an obscene bust made of real flesh and gore, it stares at you: mouth open, fear bleeding from eye sockets, defeated. You have won once again. Il Migliore del Mondo, again, your latest hunter becomes prey for your latest portrait.

***

Your latest portrait is ready. Violet, crimson, obsidian paints blur with charcoal lines. The head is alive in color, contrasting the actual subject, eye sockets staring out the window into the distance, inanimate like puckered, bruised fruit used as still life. You stare at the masterpiece, cloaked in the early morning darkness, the candles across the room casting light upon your features—you smile like a man fulfilled with destiny, like a man who has created beauty out of nothing, like God.

Il Migliore del Mondo, would you paint God's portrait if you could stare into His face? Would His radiance prove inviting when Santa Muerte, in contrast, desires only those like her—like the killer whose head sits on the mantle before you, slain like the prize of a deity and not a painter? Il Migliore del Mondo, would you roam mass graveyards and warzones to inspire enough paintings to fulfill the hunger of legions?

You cover the painting. You take the head off of the mantle. You take it to an adjacent room— your shrine, your charnel house. There, beside another desiccated head, you place your latest subject on a velvet-lined enclave. You light a candle in the room and you behold a roomful of heads, trophies—subjects. The smell of rot, clotted blood and gore nearly drives you into a frenzy.

***

What madness fancies the face of Death for a portrait? In the cold wash of sublime darkness, you light candles in your studio, enacting ritualistic craft. The paint brushes dipped in black blood graze the canvas, leaving streaks of muck, grime and humus; broad brushstrokes create the consistency of black ash and niter. The portrait comes alive in

Death's specter. Suddenly, you remember. The spade plumbs dark earth. Earthworms ooze out of the ground. The hoe splinters the casket. You open it. You take a machete and decapitate the corpse, taking your trophy.

This latest subject belongs to an old, wealthy aristocrat. He died in his home after suffering a heart attack. He was a reputed pedophile. He was famous once.

The portrait features dark hues mixing with swathes of black paint. Deep blue hues accurately depict the early stages of decomposition. Empty eye sockets gleam with the obsidian.

When the skull bears the weight of steel striking bone, the resulting cavity reveals the dead, pulpy flesh of a brain. Then, the shriveled lips divulge a slew of transgressions—a lifetime's worth of secrets.

The oral cavity, the mouth leading into forever, might have tasted a boy's innocence, stolen like it were candy. In its throat area, there was stillborn breath. In its purple tongue, there was a prison, where faces, genitalia, hands, arms, legs, colored the taste buds, trapped the memories of the rich paedophile's many victims.

The most distinct aspect of your painting lies in the man's amulet, consisting of bones, carved serpents, beaks and a small red chamber used to house his victims' blood. The paedophile would cut the boys' palms and place the blood in his amulet after the abuse. He wore their blood as protection from police, enemies. The amulet was sold to the paedophile by a voodoo priest.

Il Migliore del Mondo, you behold this painting with admiration and not revulsion, freeing this pervert's victims with an unlikely act of revelation. Are you a hero for the less fortunate, for the same townsmen and villagers who fear you? Do you choose to slay only the wicked? Do you judge as though Santa Muerte, herself had hand-picked you? Are you a savior or a sinner? Liar or prophet?

By painting this rich paedophile's portrait wearing his amulet, you trap his soul in canvas and paint. Santa Muerte would be proud, Il Migliore del Mondo. You are her instrument, her handmaid, her harvester of damned souls.

In the charnel house, you set the prize of the night's hunt in an enclave beside a trophy from another midnight odyssey. You have painted both in the light of a waning moon.

***

Your trend of ridding the city of illicit entities goes on, your next victim is the paedophile's voodoo priest. In a poor village by a swampland, you approach like funeral mist. The priest senses your arrival, defies Santa Muerte's decree of death. He mutters an unintelligible malediction and clutches at his bone necklace.

"Portador de la muerte que la muerte te tome." Bringer of death let death taketh thee.

When you appear before him from the mist, cloaked in black, armed with your stiletto, he runs into his primitive dwelling and searches frantically for his doll. You know better. You move with the speed of darkness and spear his belly with your hungry dagger. You've only hurt him, but not fatally. You take him with you to the woods to enact an ancient rite.

Deep in the foreboding woods, with swamp fetor entering your nostrils, you savor the night's sacrifice with great fervor. You've bound the voodoo priest along the wrists and ankles and tied each limb to a tree, stretching his arms and legs taut like a medieval torture rack. Il Migliore del Mondo, you pull at the contraption consisting of knotted ropes and all the man's extremities are pulled beyond their limits, dislocating joints, rupturing flesh and ligaments, tearing at the skin and exposing the muscle and bone.

The voodoo priest screams in agony and asks what he has done wrong. "Santa Muerte porque me has abandonado?" Santa Muerte, why have you abandoned me?

The wrong question, you think, obviously. Santa Muerte has designated a form of suffering worse than any excruciating torment on earth. No man may defy her decree. Priest or not.

You take your ceremonial dagger and drive it into his heart: the priest's heart ruptures, blood, voodoo potion, fear, emptiness, despair. With that voodoo potion spilled from his aorta, he turns mortal and slowly starts to die. He screams in agony; blood spatters violently from his veins. His shrieks resound on the higher register, echoing throughout the swamplands and cursed villages. The villagers are scared, not happy, despite being liberated. Once the priest is dead, you take your easel which you've stashed away until you've completed the ritual torture. You take your tubes of paint and your paint brushes and you capture the voodoo priest's violent death on canvas. Santa Muerte would be more than proud. She would applaud and the angels in hell would rejoice!

***

You have a volunteer for your next painting.

He attempts to commission you for a portrait. He arrives at your manor and calls you from the gate. He rings the bells and waits, but you do not answer. His intentions are obvious; like malodorous fumes, they cannot escape your keen senses. He wants you to kill a rival businessman and paint his portrait in all its putrid, violent glory.

You dare not do as he pleases, for you only please Santa Muerte. You defy any mere mortal that seeks Santa Muerte's favor without her blessing. Santa Muerte's image sits before you in your shrine, gifted with trophies made of heads. Every day, you bring her flowers from pestilent, miasmal waters. She stares at you—a skull robed and crowned with a tiara of flowers. She smiles as though she misses you—like your departed lover used to. She's taken her place now. Santa Muerte is best served devotedly, else would her jealousy condemn you. Therefore, you travel with the speed of darkness to the businessman's house on a hill—a mansion, a fortress protected by armed guards and dogs. You breach the perimeter via a sewage tunnel in the woods far from detection—a tunnel no man can stand for its putrid odor.

Once you climb out of a drainage port in his residence, you seek out the darkest rooms until the coast is clear. Armed guards walk by you in hallways where they cannot see, cannot smell the sewage in your black clothing because you enchant them.

Undetected, you breach the rich man's room and find him sleeping. You place your hand above his face, then smother him while he resists. Unable to breathe, he chokes on the filth on your hands, suffocates while he savors the toxic odor. You take your hand away at the last minute and let him gasp for air before cutting out his tongue so he cannot scream.

You shove a tube under his skin, in his femoral artery and you place a palette underneath it. Blood drains quickly and he loses color very fast. You take out a roll of yellow Manila paper from your tote bag, dip your fingers in his blood and paint his face. The guards and guard dogs have no idea. You have Santa Muerte's blessing, after all. He dies as his blood quickly drains. The hideous look on his face is captured in crimson swathes and smudges.

Another night, another painting. Another head goes into your trophy room. You have enough paintings to fill a showroom. You never attend the events. Your agent wires you the funds from New York City, where the paintings fetch for good prices.

You've had your fun. You dispose of the evidence from your person. Your gore-caked fingernails fresh from a night's grave robbing are scrubbed free of clot and debris. You burn your stained garments. You burn incense in your studio to rid yourself of the scent. The locals know what you do, how you do it, but not why or how.

All they know is that you are the best artist to serve Santa Muerte the world has ever seen.

***

You roam around the streets again, unburdened by the demands of your craft. The locals fear you, part like the red sea on a road where children play. Food sells in wheeled carts at odd hours and men drink outside pubs and bars. You smile back at them.

You are Il Migliore del Mondo. The locals cater to your needs. Like offering sacrifices, they offer gifts to spare them of the same fate you bestow their dead relations.

You move like a shadow on the water, like smoke on a gravel road. You walk with the grace of a schooled gentleman. Slowly, you tread the streets to your destination—the cemetery, where no prize awaits this time.

That cemetery—that grave surrounded by a dark tarn and lush gardens. Cherubims stand watch over lonely sepulchers. Nothing moves on the calm waters. The scent of Chrysanthemums fills the air.

In your mind, you recall Caccini's, Ave Maria. You hear the splendor of a soprano's soothing crescendo. As you draw closer, you also recall a woman's laughter. She resides in that grave. She knows you come every night searching for her, seeing her face transposed against the faces of victims.

But, you never extricate the prize—the same one you take from the graves of locals. This grave belongs to your deceased wife. You can't leave her for your native country. But how could you leave her now?

Instead, you imagine her beautiful face as it used to be, never similar to the putrescent heads of corpses you've taken from graves and used as models for portraits. Never the listless expressions etched in the gore of dead flesh. Never feverish souls in living flesh free to join you for the moment you find irresistible to pressure—and pleasure. Never the moment you fantasize the portrait being alive—smiling, like your wife once used to, like she never will now.

Inside the Walls

Chris Rodriguez

Bethany, exposed outside the walls, squirmed in discomfort. Her friend Alden sat with her on the bus bench. It was better than being alone. She was never alone behind the walls. At 4:00 a.m., the streets were somewhat quiet. Even the usual night owls and insomniacs were settled somewhere off the beaten path.

"So, are you ready yet?" he probed. "We've been talking for several months now. Do you trust me?"

Bethany sighed and shrugged, but said nothing.

"Where do you live?" prompted Alden.

Bethany struggled to find words. She pulled at a button on the front of her blouse. "In the walls," she whispered.

"How do you get out?"

"Jackie helps me. She tells me when I need to come out to get our checks and medicine."

"Why doesn't Jackie come herself?" Alden coaxed.

"She's afraid," Bethany stated and gave Alden a look that said, "Duh."

"You're not afraid?"

"Not if it's dark enough."

"Why do you come out only at night?"

"Because Jackie says it's too dangerous during the day."

Alden waited for more, but when it didn't come, he started again. "What would happen if you didn't help Jackie?"

Bethany shivered. "She wouldn't survive without me. She'd die."

"Can you do something for me?" Alden shifted to better see Bethany's face. She wouldn't look at him. She shrugged again, her eyes averted.

"I want you to look at something over there in that store window. Can you do that for me?"

"I guess," Bethany said as she gave the button a sharp tug.

Alden guided her toward the shop window and asked her to stand on a small crate. Bethany hesitated, then stepped up. She stood in front of the showcase window of Giselle's Garden Boutique. There was a new sun dress on display inside. She shifted a bit on the crate. If she was in just the right position, her reflection was perfectly superimposed so it looked as if she was wearing the dress. Her face was even layered over that of the store model. She frowned. Bethany had never liked her face. She thought it was much too round for her slender body type.

"What do you see?" Alden pressed.

"I see me wearing that dress," said Bethany. She couldn't take her eyes off how pretty she looked in it.

"Look again. *Is* it you?"

"Who else would it be?" snipped Bethany. "It's not Jennifer Lopez."

"Let me try something else real quick." Alden pulled an object from his pocket. "Are you okay?"

"Why wouldn't I be?" said Bethany with some trepidation. "It's almost time to go home, though," she reminded him. "So, whatever you're going to do, hurry up."

Alden hesitated for a few ticks of precious time, then stepped up to the shop window and stroked a few deft lines with a marker around the reflection on the glass. He moved back to stand close to Bethany on the box. "Now what do you see?" He watched her with expectation.

After a moment, a look of surprise and horror widened Bethany's eyes. Her mouth dropped in shock.

She couldn't quite grasp what she was seeing in the double reflection. She squinted in disbelief. She was inside Jackie's 412 lb body, looking through Jackie's eyes. A wave of vertigo rocked her, but Alden held fast to her elbow.

"Wha...?" She croaked. "How did you...?" But then the reflection was gone. The image changed as a street light was extinguished by the dawn timer.

Bethany stood still a bit longer, perplexed, then stepped gingerly off the crate. "It's time to go home," she said, urgently. "Jackie needs to help me get back into the walls."

Dr. Alden nodded. "I know," he conceded. "But next time, I'd like to talk to Jackie myself. It's time for her to come out, too."

Bethany thought about it, then nodded, "Maybe." She glanced to the east and noticed a luminous gray streak paint itself across the sky just above the soft purple hills. Bethany drew a deep breath and began the journey back to where she lived – buried in the walls.

Chrysalis

Robert Allen Lupton

The package looked like the post office used it for a hockey puck on a day when the rink in the park was dirty slush brought on by early spring temperatures and a Saturday of little league games. The string was stained black, the paper torn and dirty and there was glob of filth in one corner I told myself was either mud or a melted candy bar.

The delivery man wore plastic gloves and said, "You have to sign. The name and address were barely legible and the guys bet me a beer I'd never make this delivery. You are Brian Burkett, aren't you?"

I confirmed my name, signed, and carried the package between one finger and my thumb. I limped on my old knees to the kitchen sink, put a plastic bag over my hands and washed the package with a sponge. The shipping label was faded and smeared, but I could read my last name and the street address. The shipper's information wasn't legible. I tore the package open and saved the label.

Three layers of plastic grocery bags were sealed one after the other and inside the third layer was a dirty water stained book entitled "Chrysalis" by Walt Whitman. This had to be a joke. Rumors about the book's existence abound among bibliophiles. His rivals claimed Whitman wrote dark poetry, reputed to be black magic. He bound his evil spells,

83

enchantments, and rituals to summon demons in the self-printed and self-published volume in my hand.

One of my fellow book collectors no doubt created this forgery and sent it to me. The volume was probably a copy of "A Christmas Carol" with a carefully crafted cover. On close inspection, the design wasn't embossed and stamped on the age-darkened leather, it looked like it was printed, but the letters weren't consistently shaped. I gently peeled back a small tear. The lettering and image were visible on both sides of the leather. It reminded me of a tattooed lampshade in a Holocaust museum.

I opened the book. The title page and table of contents matched the binding. There was no information about the publisher, publishing dates, or the printer. The letters were slightly fuzzy and the rusty brown ink was blurry on the rough textured paper. I gently flipped through the book and the pages were uncut. I liked old books bound in signatures. I counted the signature groupings and they were eight pages each. I was excited that previous owners hadn't cut the pages apart. I could separate them as I read. I love the ritual and I feel awe and honor when I free a book and allow it to fulfill its destiny. For me to cut open an uncut signature is to have the opportunity to welcome a traveler from the past. Here was an entire uncut book. I sat down and calmed my breathing. I wanted every cut to be perfect. These pages are sleeping beauties, enchanted and waiting for a future prince to awaken them with the caress of a knife or razor blade.

I selected the first uncut signature, inserted my razor blade behind page five and slowly cut outward. The crisp rasp of the blade slicing the paper was better than the sizzle of frying bacon and I closed my eyes for a moment to savor it.

My hand was damp. I didn't want to stain the book with my sweat and I opened my eyes so I could find a towel. It wasn't sweat, it was blood. A vertical slice ran from my elbow to my wrist and the blood dripped from my fingers into the open book. Christ, I'd ruined a self-published and virtually unknown book written and printed by an American icon. If I didn't bleed to death, I'd kill myself.

I pressed a clean towel to my arm and wrapped it with packing tape to hold it in place. I was more concerned about the book than my arm. The book closed when I put it down. I got myself clean towels and reopened it. I wanted to dab away as much blood as I could. The pages were completely dry except for quarter-sized spots of blood on pages six and seven.

The spots shriveled into nothing in seconds. The book was warm to my touch. I didn't cut open any more pages, but the one signature was sliced cleanly open and the poetry on the exposed two pages described a ritual for the restoration of youth requiring human blood and the recitation of the enchantment inscribed on page six. Mr. Whitman, I thought, we hardly knew you.

I read page six out loud, closed the book and drove to the emergency room. The nurse unwrapped my makeshift bandage. The long scar on my arm stood white and healed on my skin. The nurse said,

"This isn't funny. This scar is over twenty years old. Are you insane? Go home. We've plenty of sick and injured people to see without bullshit like this."

I mumbled an apology, paid the bill and hurried home. The book called to me. I could hear it.

The pristine pages contained in the signature I'd cut open were blank. The uncut signatures in the small leather-bound volume were printed on the two outside pages of each section and I could peek at the interior pages without cutting them apart and see printing inside. I read page nine which described what I would find when I opened the next two pages. Inside was a healing spell. It required cremation ashes to be stirred into my blood and the mixture poured into the open book.

I rubbed the scar on my arm. I didn't feel any younger and wasn't inclined toward another bloodletting. I locked the book in a cabinet drawer.

I couldn't sleep. I told myself there was nothing supernatural about the book. Somehow I must have cut my own arm and the dry brittle pages absorbed the blood. I remembered a story where an old book contained mold spores which caused hallucinations when inhaled. I almost convinced myself, but I touched my arm and the scar was mute testimony to the contrary.

I must have finally slept because I woke to the sound of loud and regular thumping. Bang, bang and bang again. The bumps were three or four seconds apart. Smoke. I smelled smoke. I held a shirt over my nose and mouth with one hand and carried my knife in the other.

86

The thumping came from my study, but it stopped when I went inside. A blackened and fire-scorched lock lay on the floor. The drawer was open and empty. The book was centered on my desk. I turned on all the lights and unlocked and locked the doors.

My heart beat louder than the thumps which awakened me. I couldn't go back to sleep. I washed my face and filled my hand with shaving cream. I looked at the man in the mirror who looked a lot like me except his hair was black and full. His whiskers weren't the grizzled gray stubble I shaved every morning. The familiar wrinkles around my eyes were gone. I lifted my arms in the Charles Atlas pose and my triceps were tight and firm. My stomach was flat and I felt the return of vanished desire and strength in my loins.

Youth restored, indeed. No arthritis pain in my now nimble fingers. I dressed and ate breakfast. I reassured myself that I'd left my unfinished coffee in the kitchen. I couldn't bear it if I spilled coffee on a rare book.

My knees creaked when I stood and I smiled at the realization that my youth restoration didn't include new cartilage. The chunk missing from my earlobe was still gone and my right arm didn't quite straighten where a childhood broken bone healed badly. I opened the book to the next uncut section and read the healing spell which required my blood be mixed with a dead man's ashes.

My parent's ashes were in urns serving as bookends in my bookcase. I added four tablespoons of my father's ashes to a porcelain coffee cup, rolled up my sleeve and tried to figure out what to do next. Should I cut myself and bleed into the cup before I sliced open the signature or should I slice open the pages first? If this worked like last time, cutting the pages would cut me as well and I didn't want to do that twice. I slid my knife between the pages and cut about a quarter of an inch.

A ragged cut appeared in my left forearm. Small puffs of ash popped into the air as each drop of blood splatted into the cup. My eyes teared with the pain. This was too slow. I held the book down with my left elbow and balanced my bleeding arm over my father's ashes, slid the knife between the pages and sliced the signature completely open.

Blood gushed from my arm and the cup filled in seconds. I held my bleeding arm over the open book and the droplets hit the brittle pages, spread for a moment and then vanished like water drying on a windblown sheet.

I silently read the incantation and the instructions. I stirred the cup of ash infused blood and placed the spoon on the book. The blood flowed from the spoon as a river flows to the sea. I held the cup in my right hand and recited the chant.

I'd lost a lot of blood and was lightheaded. I almost dropped the cup and decided to set it aside until I needed it. I made three false starts. The blood dripped from my bandaged arm in a steady stream. My head spun. I lost my place and started over for the fourth time. Slowly, I told myself, slow and steady wins the race.

I finished the chant and almost spilled the cup of blood when nausea racked my body. I braced myself with my bleeding arm and emptied the cup into the thirsty pages. The book drained every drop until the inside of the cup was clean and dry. My arm slowly healed and the splatters of blood across the table and floor sought each other, formed rivulets and flowed into the book.

I closed my eyes until the room stopped spinning. The bandage was clean and dry. The open pages were blank and a faded old scar ran the length of my strong young forearm. My knees were pain free and, when I looked in the mirror, my earlobe was complete and there was only a thin white line to show the restored flesh.

I closed the book, but I didn't lock it away. "I won't lock you up, but I'll be gone for a while. I trust you'll be safe while I'm away."

The book answered by closing itself. The leather cover began to glow and a few tendrils of smoke curled upward as the table top began to smolder. The book stopped glowing and the old blackened leather was cool to the touch.

"I'll take that as a yes." I grabbed my coat and picked up my hat. I touched the top of my head, smiled at the feel of the thick black hair, and threw my hat on the couch. It was time for me to buy a younger man's clothes.

Dinner that night was food I hadn't been able to eat for twenty years without acid reflux keeping me up all night. I drank a bottle of red wine. I toasted the book with a double shot of whisky and went to bed.

I woke after midnight with a hangover and a dry mouth, craving water. I slid my feet out of bed and searched for my slippers in the dark. My foot recoiled when it touched something on the floor. It skittered from underfoot. My knife was on the bedside table and I opened it. I gingerly put my feet back on the floor and something bumped three times against my left foot. I jerked away, held the knife overhead, and turned on the light.

The book lay open on the floor. I didn't bring it into the bedroom. I'd left it in my study. Had I blacked out? Did the whiskey and wine fetch it here without my knowledge? That must be what happened. Drunk makes its own decisions. A stupid old man should know better than to drink so much.

I looked at the vigorous young man in the mirror when I filled my water glass. I'd been an old man once and I probably would be again, but not today. I picked up the book and returned it to the study. I tried to put it on the table, but my fingers wouldn't let go. My mind yearned for the book with the same intensity a cast adrift sailor wishes for fresh water.

I broke into a sweat and my body trembled. My heart pounded in my chest, but I forced myself to put the book down. The air was cool on my sweat-drenched skin and my heart slowed in my chest. I backed out of the study and sat in my cracked and worn recliner. I touched the aluminum softball bat on the right side of the chair and put my pocket knife on the lamp table. I wanted to hold the book with every fiber of my being, to caress its soft leather and to inhale the clean scent of the ancient handmade paper. I left the lights on and told myself not to sleep.

The sun was in my eyes and the book was in my lap. I lingered in the semi-erotic languor between awake and asleep. The book moved slightly and I swear it caressed me. I grabbed the book and stood quickly, ashamed and pleased at my arousal.

How the hell did the damn book get in my lap? Was I sleepwalking or did I simply go get the book and not remember it? I put the book in the study, showered, dressed and made coffee and oatmeal. My mind stayed with the book while I ate. It was physically painful to be separated from it. My fingers ached to trace the faded letters and butterfly illustration on the cover. The false eyes on the butterfly's wings watched everything I did. I could feel it.

I emptied the last of my coffee in the sink and hurried to the study, opened the book and buried my nose between two uncut sections. It smelled like a springtime rain shower on fresh mowed hay. It promised rebirth, warm sunshine and clear summer nights. My mind panted with desire and I wanted to climb inside the pages.

When I put the book back on the table, it opened itself to the next uncut signature, pages thirteen through sixteen. There was a hand drawn illustration of a beautiful woman. Her expression showed wisdom in the ways of love. Was she Lilith, Cleopatra, Helen of Troy, or perhaps the whore of Babylon? Perhaps she was all of them. Her body promised the ability to deliver the pleasures her face implied.

I could barely contain myself and read the words printed in faded brown below the pictures. What was the price? I had to know.

The ritual described was short and simple. Cut open the signature and recite the incantation. Of course, the book wanted my blood, but this time it also demanded a finger.

I slammed the book shut and stepped from the table. "Whitman, you bastard. A finger. You want a finger." I reread page thirteen. It didn't actually promise the woman. It promised pleasures untold. I assumed it meant the woman, but it wasn't clear. If I cut off a finger, would the woman appear? Would I turn into the woman, or would some strange erotic creature from a dark Lovecraftian nightmare crawl from inside the pages?

I was strong and resisted the book until sunset. I healed immediately after completing the first two incantations and I was damn happy with my newfound youth and healing. One finger wasn't that much and it might even grow back. Time to rock and roll.

I spread my left hand on page thirteen and cut the pages apart like pulling a bandage from a hair-covered arm. Fast is best. The pages parted and my little finger was severed at the same instant. It didn't bleed immediately and there was no pain. Shock and surprise, I suppose. I picked up my finger, opened the cut pages and placed it reverently in the gutter between pages fourteen and fifteen.

The stump on my hand bled profusely onto the pages, the pain flashed brightly behind my eyes and I screamed. I didn't pull my hand away and I let my blood flow into the book.

The incantation was short, only one couplet in length and I recited it correctly the first time. My little finger melted into red and white slurry and disappeared, bones, fingernails and all into the thirsty pages. The stump healed immediately and the pain vanished, but my finger didn't grow back.

The book blurred and the pages rippled and flowed. It looked like cats fighting underneath a blanket. Two hands reached upward followed by long smooth arms. The hands braced themselves on the tabletop and pushed downward. A woman's face rose from the book and she was more beautiful than the drawing. She wiggled and shifted, but didn't immediately climb from the book. One foot appeared and then the other. She forced her feet into the room and her legs followed. She bent almost double when her hips and waist came into view. Lastly, she pushed with her feet and elbows and levered her breasts and shoulders from the table. The book was gone, but she was here.

I was speechless. She stretched as though waking from a long sleep and smiled. She touched my young face and said, "Thank you. You have no idea how long I've been in that damn book." She kissed me and my knees went weak. I trembled like a child.

She broke the kiss and said, "The knight who rescues the princess always gets a reward. I haven't been with a man in a long time."

We didn't leave the study the first time and we made it into the hallway for the second time. After the third time, I marveled at the resilience and recovery powers granted to the unappreciative young. I caressed her back during a respite and traced the lettering and butterfly from the leather book covering tattooed between her shoulder blades. I asked her about it and she put her finger over my lips and gave me more interesting things to think about.

She was gone when I woke. The book was on the table in my study. I was terrified for a brief moment that it was only a dream, but my missing finger convinced me otherwise.

I skipped breakfast and didn't bother to dress. I opened the book; twenty uncut signatures remained. I counted them from the edges, the book wouldn't open and let me see the first page of any section except the first uncut one. The next incantation was identical with yesterday except for the price. Today's ritual required a toe, not a finger. A bargain, I thought, and put my foot on the open book and sliced the signature without hesitation. I winced at the sharp pain, but the bleeding stopped within seconds.

I helped the woman climb out of the book and followed her to my bedroom. The butterfly tattoo on her back was brighter and the eyespots on the wings stared at me.

I woke in the predawn darkness and answered the call of the book. I was shaking by the time the woman took my hand.

The next six days were a fuzzy blur. I dove headfirst into the bacchanalian celebration of depravity without reservation. On the ninth day, Delilah, I called her Delilah, fed me twice.

"Brian, you haven't eaten in over a week. You must stay strong for your Delilah. To not eat is to die." I argued and said food was a waste of time, but in a moment of clarity I looked in the mirror and my blood-bought youth was an emaciated skeleton in need of a shave. I shaved and ate the food she offered.

"You must take better care of yourself. If you die, I'll be alone." She stroked my cheek and whispered, "You don't want me to be alone."

I said, "I can't bear the thought." I spent the rest of the day showing her it was true.

On the tenth morning, I took a physical inventory. I had four fingers, my thumbs and five toes remaining. What happens after they're gone? I could survive without toes, but without fingers and a thumb, I wouldn't be able to dress or feed myself. There was one more signature remaining in the book than I had digits remaining. The book only allowed me to see one signature at a time, so I didn't know what incantation the last signature hid inside its pages.

Delilah wouldn't tell me. She said she didn't know. "My purpose is to make you happy. I do make you happy, don't I?"

I thought about how happy she made me and with that thought I found myself standing in my study and reaching to open the book. Damn, I responded to the call of the book without realizing

I'd done so. The knife was in my hand. The book wanted another finger and I wanted another day with Delilah. I cut open the next signature.

I tried to eat, but lost more weight. I have no idea how much blood the book took each time, but I know I didn't eat enough to replace it. My mind was clouded and I couldn't focus on any thoughts not related to the book and Delilah. I never answered the door. The mail slid through the slot and I left it piled on the floor. I did fetch the paper; if I let it accumulate one of my nosey neighbors would check on me.

I fell twice. It's harder to walk without toes than I expected. I hit the side of the table the second time I fell and knocked out two teeth. The book scooted across the floor and caught my blood in its open pages. I spat out the teeth and watched them soften to mush and sink into the pages.

The twentieth day came and I held the knife against my palm with my remaining thumb. Once that was gone, I wouldn't be able to feed myself, wash, use the toilet, or even open a door. If the last signature didn't offer healing and restoration, my decision to open the next signature was a death sentence. I hesitated and put my knife on the open pages.

I turned to limp away and book screamed inside my mind. The compulsion was physical and debilitating. I grabbed my head in my palms and dropped to my knees. The waves of power hit me like a tsunami and the undertow pulled me closer to the book between the surges.

96

I wiped the sweat from my forehead with my arm and opened my eyes. I stood in front of the open book. I lacked the strength of will to turn away a second time. I looked into the pages, saw the shadow of Delilah's face and I was lost. I slit apart the signature, picked up my thumb between my palms, turned the page with my tongue and watched my last finger and blood disappear into the pages.

I couldn't help Delilah climb out of the book. She didn't touch my maimed hands, but led me to the bedroom by my arm. I passed out on the floor before we reached the bed. I was nauseated and disorientated when I regained consciousness. It was dark outside. There was a blood encrusted pillow under my head and a blanket over me. Delilah was gone.

I was thirsty and limped to the bathroom. It took several tries to open the tap without fingers. I let it run, it was too hard to turn it off.

The book beckoned me, but it wasn't a demanding compulsion, it was more of a polite invitation. I answered. I'd come this far, what else was there to do?

It was open to the first page of the last uncut signature. The last incantation was one of change and rebirth. The spell was called the chrysalis and it offered a period of rest, recovery and restoration followed by a new life in a new form. The price was my right hand severed at the wrist. It was an easy decision to make. I couldn't take care of myself without fingers and I was so weak, I could die at any moment. One more fall and it would be over.

It took an hour to open the knife. I held it against the table with my palm and clenched the blade between my teeth. I held the book open with both palms and held the knife in my mouth like a pirate. It took three tries to position the blade. I cut the signature and my fingerless right hand dropped onto the table.

I turned the page with my nose and used my head to roll my severed hand onto the pages. Blood flowed into the book like it was poured from a bucket. My head spun. The flow didn't slow and my wrist didn't heal. I tried to lift my arm, but it wouldn't budge. I looked for something I could use to lever myself free. What was I thinking? I couldn't use tools.

By reflex, I moved the stump of my left hand to help force my right arm from the book. My left arm stopped at the elbow. It was limp, boneless and collapsed as though a powerful vacuum pulled it inside itself. I fell and the book stayed glued to my gushing wrist. My legs turned to jelly, sagged and withdrew into my body.

I lay silently while my body deflated and poured itself into the book. I watched until my eyes retreated into my shrunken skull. I never passed out, but all sensation vanished into a grey mist.

I was lost in a fog. No, I was part of the fog. I sensed light and moved toward it. I couldn't walk without corporeal form, but I when I thought about the light I drifted toward it. There were two holes with light streaming through them. The holes were the eyespots in the butterfly tattoo. I pressed my misty consciousness to the tattoo and looked outward through the eyes.

Delilah was in the study. She wore a pair of my jeans and a faded flannel shirt. She put her face inches from the butterfly adorned cover and said, "Thank you, Brian. I know you can hear me. Pay attention, I'm only going to say this once.

"I don't know where the book came from and I don't know how old it is. I bought at an estate sale right after the Kaiser surrendered. I wonder if Wilson is still president.

"My father and I were rare book dealers. He told me the rumors about Walt Whitman and "Chrysalis", his secret book of arcane knowledge. They could be true and Whitman might have made this book and imprisoned some spirit, demon, or devil inside it. I don't know.

"Here's what I do know. Like you, I opened the book. The first two sealed signatures offered me youth and beauty. I was an old maid bookseller and I jumped at the chance. I fought the compulsion to cut open the third signature for a month before I surrendered. It was a man for me, not a woman. He was beautiful and he treated me like a queen. I lost myself in his affections and three weeks later, I slit open the last signature and the book absorbed my body and my soul.

"During my imprisonment, over a hundred people have cut open the third signature and called me forth in a manifestation of their desires. I've been a man and a woman. I appeared as the physical incarnation of their dreams.

"You are the only one who survived to cut open the last signature. I had no idea I would be freed once that happened. All the rest died during the process or found the strength to resist the compulsion. I don't know if I'm really free or not, but I'm going to live like I am.

"My advice is meaningless, but I suggest you make people happy when they summon you from the pages. Keep them alive. You freed me and maybe someone will free you. While I was in the book, I had no sensations except for what I saw through the butterfly's eyes. I wasn't aware of time and I didn't feel anything. I never slept. I was trapped with my thoughts. I thought the nothingness would never end. I hated it. The waiting, I hated the waiting

"I'll mail the book to a rare book auction house in New York City. Best of luck."

I watched her until the brown wrapping paper covered the butterfly's eyes.

I float in nothingness without form or feeling. I have to ears to hear and no mouth to speak, but I scream inside my mind and I wait. I curse the darkness and I wait.

A Lonely Place

Dorothy Davies

It's an odd fact that the morgue can be a lonely place at times. I mean, empty lonely, desperate empty, that kind of lonely. Don't quite know why that should be, it's just a place like anywhere else. Ain't it? Well, yes, I mean, I know there's bodies there, course I do. They don't do no harm just lying in their separate drawers, each one with a name on the front that sometimes matches the name on the tag, if the police done their job proper and got the right people down to say, "yes, that's him" or her, or sometimes, it, if they didn't like the person. Happens, you know. Trust me, being there when it happened. Knows all about it, I do.

You know you thinks I ain't all there and you might be right but then again I knows things that you don't. Like I knows what happens when them that don't like the dead one comes in. Ah they pretends a bit at first, "oh how sad it is, oh what a shame" and stuff like that. They signs the papers, they go outside and they say to one another "well that's it, done and dusted. Now I guess we have to bury it."

See, I been there, I hear them, I see them, I know.

I likes wandering around here in the dark, suits me nice, this does. No one to bother me, no one to tell me to get out, no one to say "you ain't supposed to be here, get yourself out." Cos you see, they

101

don't like coming here after dark. They think them bodies is gonna get up and move about and cause a few problems. Like that's gonna happen. Them bodies is shut away in them drawers and they ain't getting out to someone opens it. And who's gonna open them drawers this time of night?

Pretty damn silly if you ask me. Was you asking me? Well, I done told you anyway. So now you knows whether you wanted it or not.

I likes it in here cos it's warm and safe and I ain't gonna be attacked like I would if I was out on the streets. Makes no difference to them what's out there that I ain't got no money or stuff on me they might want. No, stuff they do want. So I creeps in here and I stays here all night walking about, thinking about them bodies in them drawers, wondering if I open one, would someone get out and talk with me a while, just give me sommat else to think about in the long night of dark and empty and desperate when I think I would give just about anything to talk to a human being.

I'm trading safe and warm for lonely. Well, tis better than having my head bashed in and ending up in one of them drawers with a made up name on the tag which don't match the one on the front, seeing as no one around here knows who I am. So, right glad I am you dropped by tonight so we could have a talk.

Well, I thought we would talk but here is me blathering on and you saying nowt. Come on, you must have sommat to contribute. Right?

Thought so. You're scared, you're one of them that shouldn't be here cos you don't like it. So tell me this, how come you're here? How come you got through that fire door that I know well I jammed solid so no one could get in? Oh I undo it before I go, wouldn't be fair to the staff to be trapped in here with a fire, would it? It's just that when I'm here at night I like the door locked proper, then I knows I'm safe. I mean, what if one of them out there saw me come in and thought it would be a lark to follow me in?

You gonna talk to me or what?

Looks to me like it's 'or what,' not a word gone past your lips.

Here, is you real? Or is you one of those ghost people what I do hear about and never did believe in? Prove it to me, shake hands.

Well now, would you be looking at that! Went right through me that did, that hand of yours about a substantial as a smoker's breath on the last drag of a ciggie. Right then, which of them drawers is you? Oh, that one. Interesting. Not sure if I should tell you, all right I will. You was one of them where they said 'it'. Didn't they like you? You look so sad, tells me they didn't. Hold on a minute, you was that suicide, wasn't you, the one what threw himself off the bridge? Well now, if I had relatives like that, think I'd have done the same thing. Don't blame you in the least.

Listen, it's getting on for dawn. One or other of us had best be gone, better still, both of us better be gone before the staff arrives.

Which way you going? I mean is you gonna leave here or is you gonna hang around with your body? Ain't a lot of good to you, is it?

103

Wanna come with me? I got this nice place under the bridge, got me a little den there, brew up some coffee and if I'm lucky a bit of toast in front of me fire. You're welcome to share. Serious I am, we can share, because you don't seem to realise we're both on the same side of life, mate. Just cos your hand went through mine didn't mean I'm alive and you're not. Your hand went through mine cos I'm a ghost, too. Ha! Your face! You thought I was a human and could see a ghost, right? Well, I like to play that trick on people, works every time. And you fell for it!

This morgue can be a bit of a lonely place at times, see, you need a funny trick or two to pass the time. It's been a few years since I had someone to talk to.

Right glad I am to meet you.

Coming?

Blinding a Few Dogs

Gary Budgen

He thinks, as a consequence of this, that it may be possible to live visually in one part of the world, while one lives bodily in another. He has even made some experiments in support of his views; but so far, he has simply succeeded in blinding a few dogs.
"The Remarkable Case of Davidson's Eyes" by H.G. Wells

The advertising billboard across the dual carriageway had been vandalised again. The poster, made up of six rectangular sections, never stayed intact for very long; the local kids would tear at it, pull away pieces. No, the upper portion was for a Hollywood movie and a woman with ice blonde hair in a low cut white dress stared out; just where her cleavage plunged the poster had been ripped off to show the bright yellow sands of a tropical island from some holiday dream of months ago.

Avery stared at the poster. There was a problem with his left eye. His vision had become partially obscured by an obstruction shaped like a curved diamond, a little smudge filled with ambient colour. Around this his sight was unaffected, it was this small area that had gone wrong. The diagnosis was macular degeneration. The cells of his macula had become damaged and the condition would get gradually worse so that eventually it would affect both eyes, although the rate of decay could vary between them. The day Avery came back from the doctors with the diagnosis he knew he would have to make the most of his time left because soon he might no longer be able to see Jennifer.

He sat in his armchair at the window and looked out over the dual carriageway. Apart from the smudge he could still see everything clearly. There was the billboard and the endless succession of mostly silver-grey cars under the gaze of the speed cameras. Beyond the dual carriageway was a row of houses, almost identical to the row this side where his own house was. Many had doors and windows boarded up and even those houses still inhabited were dilapidated with the paint flaking off their badly clad fronts. Cheap rents for those with no-where else to go. There was nothing beautiful here at all. Only Jennifer was beautiful.

He sat this way until dusk, watching the car headlights come on with their drowsy distant glow. When he woke, still in the armchair, the traffic had dwindled. Avery looked around the room and knew he should clear up. Soon he might be blind and didn't want to trip over the boxes of returned packages that Jennifer had sent back, the soft toys, the chocolates and lingerie. On the coffee table a stack of letters from the police and the court had slid into an untidy pile. Perhaps, after all, not seeing all of this might actually be a relief.

In bed he thought, as always, of Jennifer. The first time he had seen her had been in the newsagent in one of the little streets beyond the dual carriageway. He often went to that newsagent because it wasn't too close to his house and was usually empty. He would be in and out quick, grabbing one of the magazines and paying for it without really checking it was one that he would like.

This time *she* had come in and Avery knew there was an instant attraction. He had stood by the little carousel of birthday cards and watched as she'd gone to the counter.

"Hello, Jennifer," the shopkeeper had said.

She'd bought cigarettes while Avery took in her back, her black hair, the shape of her body in the track suit.

He'd followed her home that day.

***

In the morning the smudge in his eye had changed. In shape and size it was the same but there was something about the light and colour that was different. He lay back on his bed and tried to examine it.

It had become darker, yet not quite black. The light had changed and what had been an obstruction was now a crack he could see into. The crack darkened with shadow; then lightened again. This reoccurred without any regular interval. The shadow sometimes covered the whole of the crack and sometimes only part of it, making odd darker shapes against the grey.

Avery lay and watched and at last realised that the flittering shadow was in fact something moving. He tried to focus as though his own eye might look through that part of itself that was this crack. But then the moving shadow was gone and the crack became what it had been before, coloured the same dull magnolia as his bedroom walls and ceiling.

By the time Avery got up it was mid-morning; too late to see Jennifer on her way to work. But he could make it for when she came out to lunch. He left the house, finding it easier to close his left eye as much as possible rather than being distracted by the crack. He got a few strange glances on the bus but soon it had dropped him further up the dual carriageway at the edge of the industrial estate where Jennifer worked as a receptionist in a print firm. Avery wasn't allowed into the estate anymore but if he stood at the entrance, over 100 yards away from the print firm entrance, he might see Jennifer when she came out to go to the little caravan that sold tea and snacks.

But today she did not emerge, even though he stood there for over an hour, the wind picking up and blowing grit onto his skin, making him close both eyes against it. Once he saw one of the other girls who worked with Jennifer. She knew who he was but ignored him.

For the afternoon he retreated via a foot tunnel to the other side of the dual carriageway where there was a row of shops and a café.

He sipped tea as the image in the crack in his eye came to life with a wavering of flickering shadow that moved from side to side and then, adding depth for the first time, seemed to move inwards away from him. Unmistakably, for a moment, the shapes became the silhouette of a human being.

"Are you all right?"

Avery must have cried out because the old waitress was stood next to his table, speaking to him.

"I'm fine," he said, looking at her only for a second.

"Well, you can't just sit there all afternoon with one cup of tea again."

He ordered another and screwed his left eye closed. As long as he could see Jennifer later it didn't matter.

After three or so hours he went over and waited again by the entrance to the industrial estate. Mercifully the crack in his left eye had become dim and grey, devoid of movement. He saw the staff come from the print firm but Jennifer wasn't with them. As they passed by, one of the men – the one called Frank – came over.

"Why don't you just fuck off?" he said to Avery.

"Where's Jennifer?" Avery asked.

The woman he had seen earlier came over; she was red-faced and when she spoke she spat the words: "You've done it now, you freak. She's gone somewhere you'll never find her."

"Where?"

"Just fuck off," said Frank.

"No," said Avery, "she wouldn't do that. She wouldn't leave me."

***

On the bus home he shook as he wondered what might have happened to Jennifer. He knew she had a difficult life, that she couldn't express what she felt about him. Avery had always suspected some man in the background, some bully. Probably Frank at the print firm. Poor Jennifer. At first she had replied to his letters and presents but then she'd begun to send them back. There had been a message: *Please. I really don't want you to bother me anymore.* But Avery had not been deceived. He knew there was some kind of duress involved.

In his armchair again, he looked out over the cars as the evening came. He would have to make sure that she was gone, go and see the house even if it meant going against the court order. The crack in his eye was dark, hardly seen but when he stood to go out a jabbing pain poked at his eye. It became so intense that he fell to his knees; but even with his eye screwed shut he could feel the crack changing, growing.

He looked.

What was there was a room. The view was larger now, the crack became a hole in which he could see objects made up of grey: a bed and a wardrobe; near the foot of the bed a chest of drawers with a chair in front of it. Beyond the bed, straight ahead, was a square of mud-coloured light contrasting with the greys of the furniture. It was a window. He was looking into a room at night.

There was still the pain and, carefully, Avery touched the surface of his eye but this only made him flinch. He needed water so he stumbled towards the bathroom, his foot catching on one of the returned packages. The pain was getting worse even as the scene he could see became more distinct so he could make out the two columns of furled up curtains either side of the window. Now the room was both light and dark, like creased silver foil. The moon was coming up outside the window. It began to burn away, searing the surface of his eye.

Avery threw the toothbrush out of its plastic beaker and filled this with water. He tipped his head back and poured the water into his eye. For a moment, as the water dribbled down his neck, the pain lessened. The room in his eye was drenched, as though beyond a wet car window screen.

***

The first time he had really looked at Jennifer he had been waiting across the street from her house. It was morning, before eight o'clock, but he had got there early in case she left for work. It had been before he found out where she worked.

She was smartly dressed in a dark trousers suit, her hair pinned up. Yes. He approved; she should dress like this rather than the track suit she had been wearing in the newsagent. He crossed the street to get behind her, noting with delight that a strand of her hair had come loose. It began to rain and she started to trot. Because the sun was still bright the rain drops sparkled on the pavement. Her hair, tightly held except for the loose strand, shone with wet light. It was one of those moments he wanted to fix. To keep forever.

At the bus stop on the dual carriageway he spoke to her.

"Hi."

She nodded at him and looked away. Then she shuffled down to the other end of the shelter.

Perhaps she was pretending not to remember him. Perhaps she was playing hard to get.

He sat two rows behind her on the bus and when she got off at the industrial estate he said goodbye. She ignored him but he noted the time and place.

***

With his eye still soaked and screwed shut, he left the house and began to walk towards the dual carriageway. There was a hospital not far away. He passed the billboard lit up for the evening. The advert had changed again to one for a brand of commercial vans. The van, a smart white box, stood proudly above the lesser vehicles passing on the road beneath it. When he reached the grounds of the hospital he dared to open his eye. The moonlight silvered the room. It hurt for a moment as he tried to make out the features: the bed in the foreground where a shape stirred. Then the pain again and he stumbled through the plastic doors of the casualty department.

They irrigated his eye and eventually the pain subsided. He kept it closed as they led him to a bed in some kind of transit room.

***

He would be outside the print firm most days, walking with her to the caravan where she got her lunch, usually some sort of sandwich, occasionally a burger.

After the first time she was never on her own, always some gaggle of other women or –worse – men in overalls. The women glared at him. The men abused him. Jennifer said nothing. He realised that everyone was trying to keep them apart, to keep her from him. It was as though she were being held captive in plain sight.

One day, one of the men attacked him, punching him and pushing him to the ground.

"Don't, Frank," Jennifer pleaded for the man to stop; trying to protect Avery.

"It's all right, Jennifer," Avery said. His head throbbed from the punch. "I'm okay."

She bent low, pushing her face towards him as though she were some long-necked beast.

"Don't you fucking see?" she said. "I hate you."

When the police came as he waited outside the print works, Avery was confused. Weren't they here because Jennifer had called them after Avery had been hit? But they put him in a cell and questioned him and the whole process that led to the court order began. The relentless interviews; the making him watch the CCTV footage of himself on the industrial estate, his fuzzy edged figure shifting his weight from foot to foot as he waited to see Jennifer.

It seemed that Jennifer's false friends had conspired to ruin everything.

***

"Mr Avery," some young man, possibly a doctor, said to him. "We're going to have to keep you in hospital. We think the condition of your eye has deteriorated rapidly."

"I can't see very well." This wasn't really true but he did not know what else to say.

"It's all right," said this doctor or whatever he was, "we have your notes. The consultant will see you in the morning."

Avery tried to focus on where he was as they led him through the hospital to a ward. There were beds with their white sheets and heads of men poking out the top. Most were sleeping in the dimmed light from the nurses' station. His left eye felt a little better and he ventured to open it. In the room inside it was night and, just like the ward, there was a shape asleep on the bed.

***

In the morning the consultant came. Within his eye, now painless, calm, what had once been the rounded diamond crack was now a much wider opening. Avery could see the room there clearly: a bedroom with someone asleep in the bed, their form hidden by blankets.

"Good morning, Mr... Avery."

Avery tried to take him in, closing off the interior room for a moment and focusing on the hospital ward. He saw a tall man in a purple bow-tie, grey and with glasses.

"I've got your notes here. I understand your vision has taken a sudden decline. You've had some pain as well?"

"They said it would become steadily cloudier, but..."

The consultant came closer and Avery just wanted him to *do* something, examine him, but he just seemed to want to ask questions.

"Yes, please go on, Mr Avery."

"There's a room..." Avery didn't know how to explain it, "and other things. I'm not going blind... I can see. Just not here. Or not only here."

"Hmm." The consultant rubbed his chin. "If I could just examine your eye..."

He leant towards Avery with his ophthalmoscope. The room was still there inside, touched by the light from the instrument as though the sun had come down too close to the Earth. On the bed the covers were stirring, being thrown back. Two slender feet and legs slid out.

"There's certainly damaged cells in the macular..."

In the morning light of the bedroom that only Avery could see Jennifer sat on the edge of the bed, yawning. She wore a ragged tee-shirt and her hair was messy but it was undoubtedly Jennifer. Avery had found her again.

"Have you had any injuries lately?" the consultant was saying, "I mean head injuries?"

"What's that got to do with my eye?"

It was hard to pay attention; he was watching Jennifer.

"Certain neurological injuries..."

In the bedroom the edges of her legs were lined with the touch of light from outside. She put her feet to the floor, the light flowing across her as she turned. Avery watched her walk towards the window.

"We can tell from the examination that the cells in your left eye have degenerated. But what I'm referring to is you saying you can see still. Is that correct, Mr Avery?"

She stood at the window. The curtains were already open and she looked out over the vast expanse of sky. She was up high somewhere. Not her old house. All the objects in the bedroom were clear, the wardrobe, the chest of drawers and chair. Mirror light played on her back where the tee-shirt just reached to the top of her legs. Then she went over to the chest of drawers and began to search for something.

"Anton-Babinski syndrome. Rather rare condition, as a matter of fact. The illusion of sight in a blind person. The brain supplying the images... That's why I asked if you'd had a head injury."

Avery was disappointed that her underwear was plain, boring. But he quickly dismissed this and focused on her, on her presence as she sat, now dressed, at the mirror and began to put on make-up.

"What I'd really like to do is keep you in for observation. There's a man... a colleague, who I think would like to talk to you. Mr. Avery? You understand what I'm saying, don't you?"

Avery ate the meals when they were brought and struggled somehow to the toilet, trying for a few minutes to remember where he was, to look at the other beds, the stands with their drip bags, the other patients. But he couldn't not look at Jennifer. He followed her from room to room. She was completely unaware of her desirability and this made him greedier for her. If only he could zoom in. If only he could taste her with his eye. The eyes were nervous tissue after all, wasn't that what some doctor or other had told him?

Although she had dressed in work clothes she never left the flat. For a while she watched daytime TV. She made a phone call in the evening but Avery couldn't hear what she said. Afterwards she lay on her bed and cried, great sobs that shook her whole body as she curled her arms around her head.

"Mr Avery, I've brought someone to see you."

It was the consultant. He stood there again, twiddling his silly bow-tie. Beside him was another man, a tall, broad man in a dark suit that matched his close cropped dark hair. He might have been in his sixties but he was still tough looking. He smiled for a moment at the consultant then stepped ahead of him, right up next to Avery's bed.

"Hello, Mr Avery," he said, "pleased to meet you. I'm Danes."

There was a quiver in his voice as though this Danes had found something slightly funny.

Jennifer was watching TV. Some old film. Avery had often thought about how their evenings might be spent when they were together. Sat close on the sofa watching something sentimental. Something she would like.

Then Danes said: "Can you see Jennifer, Mr Avery?"

"What are you talking about?" the consultant said.

"Oh," said Danes, "I think this is best left between myself and Mr Avery. Why don't you go and rustle us up a cup of tea and a biscuit? There's a good man."

For a moment the consultant hesitated, looked at Avery as though for an answer and then turned and walked away.

"Who are you?" Avery asked.

"I'm the man hospitals call when they get people like you."

"You're an eye specialist?"

Danes sat on the edge of the bed, his bulk making it sag.

"We know all about you, Mr Avery," he said. "We know all about your little brush with the law. The stalking."

Avery didn't like that word. Other people had used it. But stalkers were weirdoes. Dirty old men.

"I never did anything…"

"It's fine," said Danes, "don't be concerned. We understand perfectly. Be reassured, there's a place for you. It's going to be all right."

***

On the drive to the country Avery was only half aware of where they were going. They were in a large black car and Danes was seated in the front next to the driver. They went along the dual carriageway near to his house. The billboard had been vandalised again, the side of the white van ripped away to reveal a piece of beach, or perhaps the folds of a dress of an extremely glamorous woman from a movie. He couldn't tell if it was a person or a landscape.

He watched Jennifer as she settled down in bed, her body once again beneath the sheets as night fell. At some point, after motorways and smaller roads, the car bumped along a lane. There were lights, a gate in a high chain link fence. After the entrance buzz the driver showed a pass and a torch shone into the car.

"Sorry, Mr Danes," someone said and the car crunched down on gravel.

Jennifer slept on.

"Welcome to my domain," said Danes.

***

Avery was given a small room with a bed and a bedside table. A male warder came back after a while with a bedside light. There were bars on the windows.

Avery didn't mind. He was content to peer into his own inner darkness, the darkness of Jennifer's room, never truly dark because the curtains were left open. He studied her silhouette on the bed.

When he woke in the morning he watched as she got up and dressed. Once again she put on her smart work suit with a skirt and tights. She applied make-up carefully, slowly. She walked to the front door of the flat and Avery was suddenly alarmed. If she left, would he be able to follow her? She opened the front door. Outside was a lobby and the door to another flat opposite. Jennifer stood there holding the door jamb. Stood in the open door. She seemed to be there for a great length of time before she closed the door and went into the sitting room and slumped down on the sofa, kicking her shoes off. She held her head in her hands and cried.

"Mr Avery," said a different male warder who had come into the room, "come along. Mr Danes is going to show you round personally."

"I'm hungry." Avery realised this as he said it.

"Mr Danes will take you to the resting room. You'll be able to get some food there."

Avery followed in the pyjamas they had given him in the hospital. Danes appeared and took his elbow but Avery shook him off.

"Oh, yes," said Danes, "forgive me. I'm so used to having to help the inmates here."

"What is this place?"

"This is the Davidson Institute. We help people like you. That's why I had to get you away from those fools in the hospital. They think you're imagining your inner sight. But we know better, don't we?"

Jennifer was still crying.

"Yes," said Avery, "I know what I'm seeing is real."

"The girl?" said Danes. "Sad, really. I'm given to understand she was somewhat traumatised. Moved towns. Agoraphobic."

"I need to go to her."

"Yes," said Danes, "amazing, isn't it? And soon you'll see so much more."

Avery stopped in the corridor. He wanted to go back to his room, to watch Jennifer but this Danes might be able to help him.

"What is it? What's happening to me?"

"Well," said Danes, "we have no more real idea of how it works than we did when the Institute opened. Quantum entanglement. Sympathetic Magic. Who knows?" He laughed for a moment. "But in the end we don't worry too much about that. This is not a theoretical research facility. Our work is primarily practical."

"Practical?"

"Oh, don't worry. We don't torture dogs anymore."

"Sorry?"

"Just an in-joke. I mean we gave up long ago trying to create the effect. We just have to find the right sort of people. People like you."

He led Avery ahead through some double doors into a large open room, done out like a series of little lounges with sofas and armchairs. Warders moved about the room and Avery saw people, mostly men but a few women, sat on sofas and armchairs staring into nothing. The warders delivered trays to their laps and placed drinks in hands.

"Looks like you're just in time for breakfast," said Danes. "You see how fortunate you are. All the others here, with similar abilities to you, have gone blind in both eyes."

Danes led him over to one of the little arrangements of armchairs around a coffee table. One of the chairs was occupied by a man of perhaps Avery's age. It was difficult to tell because he was bald.

"Tom," said Danes addressing the man, "I'd like you to meet Avery. Sam Avery, isn't it? He's new here."

The man turned his head slowly towards Danes' voice and sighed as though coming out of a sleep.

"Oh," he said, "sit down. Danes always brings the new ones to me. I suspect he thinks I'm understanding or something."

"Well, I'll leave you to get acquainted then."

After Danes left, Avery hovered for a while and eventually settled in an armchair.

"I'm not staying," said Avery, "there's someone I want to see."

"Your focus?" said Tom.

"What?"

"The one you stalked. The one who set all this off."

"How do you know? What have people been saying?"

Tom raised his arms and indicated the room.

"Who do you think we all are?"

"What do they do here? Don't they help you?"

But they were all blind. All blind.

"They get to us while we can still see a little. I went to a doctor when I could just see a tiny bit of where... she was called Sally, where Sally was. I thought I was just going crazy. Well it doesn't matter. No-one missed me when they brought me here. No-one misses people like us. They show you endless photos and videos of someone they're interested in. Someone they want to keep tabs on. They give you drugs. As you begin to lose your real sight your focus shifts. You can't help it. The one I see now is a politician in Pakistan. I can't stop watching him. Watch him take a shit. Fuck his wife. But I shouldn't complain, at least he's still alive..."

Avery stood up. He had to get out of here.

"I've still got one good eye," he said, "I'm not like you."

"Oh," said Tom, "they'll find you ever so useful." He looked up at Avery with his blank dead eyes.

From the corner of the room warders were approaching, big men with heavy arms. And somewhere Jennifer was putting on her shoes; was brushing down her skirt and heading once again to the front door of the flat.

Rent Money

Rie Sheridan Rose

It didn't matter how you counted it, she was still $90 short of the rent and two weeks late besides. Mr. Andropolos had been very understanding the first time: "That's all right, Katrin. Pay me when you can. I trust you," and a little less forgiving the second: "Well, Miss Savoy, I can give you until next Tuesday, but that's the best I can do," and downright surly this month: "If I don't have my rent by Friday, I must ask you to leave."

Katrin Savoy couldn't really blame him. She wasn't sure she would put up with her excuses if their positions were reversed. It didn't help that the explanations were true.

So what if things were in a slump at work? Who cared if she'd had to replace her paid-off jalopy with a new car and its requisite insurance, delivering a deathblow to her carefully projected monthly budget? Why should Mr. Andropolos suffer because she had been rushed to the emergency room for an unscheduled appendectomy that had eaten what little cushion had been left in the bottom of her savings account?

Katrin ran distracted fingers through her long blonde hair, wincing as she caught a tangle and accidentally yanked harder than she'd intended. "God, give me a break!" she pleaded silently, but God wasn't answering His messages.

"There's got to be *something* I can do," she muttered to herself, methodically searching each room of the apartment for any portable, pawnable item that she hadn't already hocked. It wasn't much, two or three lousy CDs that nobody wanted and a couple of broken gold chains.

What the hell am I going to do?

She didn't have the figure for exotic dancing and she wasn't any good at poker. The start-up cost was too high for dealing drugs and the threat of disease too terrifying to consider hooking, though she'd always privately thought getting paid for sex had a marvelous sound to it.

Katrin sank down onto the couch, drawing her knees up under her chin and hugging them miserably. *I'm just about at the end of my rope, hanging on by the tips of my fingers and dangling above a bottomless pit.*

It was clichéd, but she couldn't afford originality.

There was a knock on the door, startling her to her feet in one jerky motion.

"Jesus, he said I had until Friday!"

She moaned under her breath and began trying and discarding excuses as she made her way to the door, so sure it was Mr. Andropolos that she stammered awkwardly when it was a complete stranger framed in the doorway. "Uh, hello. I-I wasn't expecting... I mean I—may I help you?" she finally blurted out.

"Oh no. No, no, no," the little man smiled, raising a hand as if to stop her questions and shaking his head. "I am here to help *you*."

His voice was vaguely accented and his mannerisms reminded her of a young Roddy McDowell but she couldn't remember which movie.

"Excuse me?" Katrin asked politely.

"Oh my, yes! I have come in answer to your prayers."

Katrin stared. She couldn't quite bring herself to put the full question into words. "You mean…" She pointed upward, with a dazed expression on her face.

"No, no, my dear." Suddenly he wasn't so loveable Roddy McDowell anymore. With a broad grin showing an uncomfortable number of very sharp teeth, he pointed downward.

Katrin gulped. She had never been a big churchgoer, though she did have a nebulous belief in a Supreme Being, but Hell was another story entirely. She had no doubt whatsoever about the existence of Hell.

"I see," she murmured softly, the words catching like spider webs at the back of her throat. "Well, I really don't think—"

"Yes, yes," replied the demonic messenger. "That is precisely the point, my girl. You *don't* think and so I have been appointed to do it for you. Aren't you going to invite me in?" he asked pointedly.

She hesitated. *Maybe demons are like vampires. If I don't let him in he will just go away and leave me alone.*

"Come, come, Miss Savoy. I do have other clients."

Katrin looked at the man's expensively tailored suit and custom leather briefcase.

Demon or not, he definitely had money and this was one time she was too desperate to worry about the risk. *If he wants to murder me, hey—at least I won't have to pay the rent.*

"Come on in," she sighed, stepping back from the doorway.

"Thank you." The messenger crossed the threshold with such a decisive movement Katrin decided she must be right about the need for an invitation.

What do you know, there's protocol even in Hell, she mused.

"Can I offer you anything, Mister...?" She trailed off, not having been given a name.

This whole thing is rather outside the realm of my hostessing experience.

"Mr. Iscariot will do."

"Like in the Bible?"

"You make one little mistake and it follows you through eternity." He was clearly upset.

"I'm sorry. I didn't mean to imply..."

"Of course you did. Everyone does. No one wants to hear *my* side of it. But that's neither here nor there, my girl." He sat down on the edge of the couch and opened his briefcase, glancing at a stack of papers as he spread them on the coffee table. "You know, that grapefruit soda in the refrigerator would hit the spot quite nicely," he looked up at her with a bright smile.

Katrin groaned inwardly. *I was saving that for a particularly lousy day. Those sodas always make me feel better, and they're hard to find these days. Trust him to pick the one thing that I wouldn't have freely offered. But hey, you can't deny a demonic messenger, now, can you?*

She fetched the soda and a glass and set them on the table beside his open briefcase then sank down in the chair opposite. The demon took a sip and smacked his lips. "Ahh. Delicious! Thank you, my dear."

"Umm…you're welcome."

"Now, let's see what we can do about your little financial problem, shall we?" He scanned a document, frowning thoughtfully. "Hmm, I see." He flipped the page. "And…ah." A nod, and another flip. "Oh dear, dear, dear! We have been a naughty girl."

Katrin shifted uncomfortably. "I wouldn't say that. I—"

Iscariot shot her a steely glance and she flushed. "Well, I wouldn't," she mumbled. "Thoughtless maybe, but not naughty."

"All a question of semantics pet," he soothed. "Well, I think I get the gist of it." He shuffled through his papers and slipped a form from the pile. "Here we are."

The demon placed the paper before her. "I am prepared to offer you $30 million."

"Do I get that in silver?" she mumbled, unable to resist.

"I heard that," Iscariot snarled. "It wasn't funny then, and it's still not funny."

"Sorry," Katrin apologized, face flaming scarlet.

"No one need know where the money came from and in return, you pledge your eternal soul to the Master whenever he chooses to claim it."

"Now wait a minute," Katrin protested. "How do I know he won't claim it tomorrow? What's the good in getting the money just to have it taken back again like that?"

"Clever girl," beamed Iscariot. "You do have a point. Many clients miss that one and we do pick up quite a few quick returns that way. Let's see now...."

An elegant ballpoint pen appeared in his hand. "What do you feel is a fair term for the contract?"

She looked into the future from the safety of her twenty-five years and chose a number that seemed like eternity. "Fifty years?"

"Excellent choice," he commended her, making a notation with his pen. "Enough time to have a full life but not long enough to get bored with it all."

Katrin began to relax. *He is really a very decent man. Maybe this whole thing isn't as bad as I've always been led to expect.*

"Oh!" she cried, as a thought hit her. "And put in there that 'I don't want to get old' thing. You know, the 'eternal youth' clause. I mean, your boss doesn't want a decrepit old soul, does he?"

Iscariot nodded. "Very wise. You haven't done this before have you?" he teased her.

Katrin giggled despite herself as he made another revision. *Yeah, this wasn't so bad at all. That fire and brimstone thing must be an exaggeration.*

"Now, is there anything else you can think of?" he asked politely.

Katrin shook her head.

"Fine. Here you are. If you could just sign there and initial the changes." He indicated a dotted line with the tip on his pen.

Katrin picked up the contract.

"What are you doing?" he asked, suddenly flustered.

"Don't worry. I'm just reading over the contract."

"You don't need to do that!"

"I'll sign it, don't worry. But I want to see exactly what I'm... what does this 'suffer the torments of Hell' mean?"

"Oh, that's just contractual rhetoric. Nothing to worry your pretty little head about." He made a grab for the paper and she moved it out of his reach.

"I, Katrin Elaine Savoy do hereby render to His Satanic Majesty, Lucifer—no ego on *this* being, is there?"

"Please, Miss Savoy!" Iscariot was clearly shocked.

"I'm sorry. I'm sorry. 'Do hereby render... blah, blah, blah... one soul to be collected in fifty years' time. In return, I will receive the sum of thirty million dollars and the gift of eternal youth.' Sounds like a plan to me."

Katrin signed her name with a flourish.

***

130

Fifty years had seemed like an eternity to a twenty-five year old girl, but as the end of her contract grew inexorably nearer, Katrin began to have second thoughts. She was having far too much fun to meekly acquiesce to fulfilling her part of the bargain. Oh, she had no complaints about the way the Other Party had lived up to his; she had never aged another day and — with a little careful finagling — had managed to conceal that fact from the rest of the world. But now, with slightly less than a week to go until the expected payoff, she spent every night poring over her copy of the contract, searching for a way out.

The thirty million dollars, conveniently explained away by the death of a non-existent aunt (*Oh yes, terribly sad. I was heartbroken. We were inseparable when I was a child*) had long since expanded into ten times that sum. She could easily return the money, but somehow she didn't think that was an option.

What am I going to do?

The answer came to her as she sat in the twilight shadows of Central Park, brooding over the clauses of the contract that were indelibly etched into her brain. It was so simple she smiled, then started to chortle softly and then guffaw out loud from sheer relief. The pregnant girl with the desperate eyes sitting on the bench opposite her looked over in dull surprise.

It was the opening Katrin needed. "When are you due?"

"In two weeks," the teenager replied, her voice as lifeless as her hair and eyes. The girl was no more than fourteen, all skin and bones except for her distended belly.

She looked hungry and amenable. Katrin knew that look well.

"Would you join me for dinner?" Katrin asked, rising to her feet and holding out a hand. "I'd like to tell you a little story."

She had to give the child credit. The girl frowned and shook her head, drawing deeper into her thin jacket.

"I don't think so, ma'am."

"Would you do it for a thousand dollars?"

The girl gulped. "Are you crazy?"

"No," Katrin shrugged. "Just rich." She held out her hand again, but this time it contained a folded stack of bills. "What do you say?"

The girl looked at the bills in Katrin's hand. Her soul was in her eyes. Tentatively, she reached forward, drew her hand back, then snatched the bills and stuffed them in her pocket. "Dinner. That's all."

"But, of course, dear." Katrin purred, slipping an arm around the girl's shoulder.

***

The expected knock came a few minutes earlier than Katrin had anticipated. She wasn't quite finished with her task. "Just a minute," she called out. "I'll be right there!"

This is harder than I expected, she grunted to herself, rocking the knife blade through a particularly tough bit. *Ah, there we go!* She reached inside the cavity and lifted out her prize.

132

The knock came again, more impatient in its tenor.

"I'm coming!" She swiped the damp hair from her forehead, leaving a smear of blood behind her hand.

She opened the front door. "Come in, Iscariot." She stepped back, expecting him to follow with the unconscious arrogance her money had bred in her.

Iscariot glanced at the bloody thing on the living room floor and shook his head indulgently. "Having a final bit of fun?"

"I don't think so," Katrin smirked, thrusting the squalling infant into his chest. "Here you go. Payment in full."

"What? Are you daft, girl? You signed a contract. You sold the Master your soul in exchange for a substantial amount of cash."

"Oh no, my friend. You're mistaken. Look at your contract. I promised your Master *a* soul. And there it is." She pointed a gory hand at the tiny infant, cut from its mother's womb. Her eyes glittered and she laughed the jittering laugh of one who has been to the edge of the Abyss and only come part way back. "Consider the $30 million rent money."

Becoming Witch

Olivia Arieti

The house was definitely part of the forest; made
entirely of wood, with gables and a bleak stack. It
emerged as an eerie shadow from the drooping
branches of the surrounding trees. Becky's
forefather purchased it during the infamous and
sadly famous witch hunt that occurred in the area a
few centuries ago. Rumours were it had been a
hiding place for the poor girls accused of witchcraft
and for the souls of those who hadn't been able to
escape their persecutors' hysteria.

The structure was abandoned as it was
considered haunted. Since Becky was on a tight
budget and in desperate need to spend some time
alone, she went there all the same.

The girl was heartbroken; Jason, her fiancé, had
walked out just after announcing their wedding
date. She was deeply in love and had always
accepted his whims, whether amusing or annoying,
but this time he went too far.

The guy, as handsome as vain, was a successful
attorney and more than once boasted about
descending from a dynasty of magistrates. When
Becky told him the story of the creepy house, his
face darkened; reluctantly he revealed that one of
his ancestors, a renowned judge, had taken part in
the hunts.

The hinges of the massive door, framed by strings of withered foliage, screeched angrily when Becky entered as though vexed by the intrusion.

Dust was all around, cobwebs hung from the ceiling like myriads of nets waiting to entangle her.

The place looked intriguing, though, as if the witches' magic was still working and their invisible cauldron was bubbling in the fireplace.

Many were the books about witchcraft resting on the shelves and the girl couldn't resist going through them. What seemed so occult and uncanny appeared natural, almost fun. She learned how to prepare potions and wondered if ever she would be able to cast an evil spell on Jason.

As a matter of fact, her pain was slowly being replaced by strong feelings of resentment. Despise was winning over love and, somehow, she felt released from an obscure force that sooner or later would have burnt her soul and body just like a witch at the stake.

After a fortnight of meditations and introspection, however, the silence of the forest was dismaying and the solitude a too heavy presence. The time to pack up had arrived.

Hurried knocks interrupted her preparations.

A girl dressed in black with dishevelled hair stood on the threshold. Becky stepped back.

"I didn't mean to frighten you," the newcomer said, "simply wanted to greet our neighbour," and pushed the door open.

"Actually, I don't live here and am about to go back home."

"Oh no, you can't leave without meeting the others. We organised a welcome party for you. By the way, I'm Abigail," and she stretched out her clammy hand.

The stranger's mysterious charm was too intriguing to ignore.

The girls ventured into the woods and had to make their way through the coarse vegetation while the path narrowed. Thorny shrubs pricked Becky's arms and sharp stones penetrated the soles of her boots. For sure, the new adventure looked more dreary than exciting.

"Hey, this is a cave," when they arrived.

"Where did you think witches live, doll, in a castle?"

A dark room opened before her; a decrepit cupboard, benches, stools and a charred table were the only furniture. A greasy cauldron stood in the centre of the fireplace and a dozen of broomsticks were heaped in a corner.

At once, a group of barefoot girls in rags emerged apparently out of nowhere.

"These are my sisters, hon, the ones hanged or burnt in the hunts; fire has incinerated their souls and horror turned their blood black. The devil himself led them to this cave."

Becky gazed at her. Were they ghosts? Was her hostess a ghost as well?

She added, "I've been spared, but at the sight of their tortures and death, evil began nourishing my soul; at the end, my blood turned black too and I was admitted to their cave."

Maybe it was all a horrid nightmare... Could she have fallen while packing up and hit her head?

"Let's greet our guest properly," exhorted a girl with eyes blacker than octopus ink.

"She was the youngest to be hanged," Abigail said. "The signs of the rope are still visible on the neck bones, a truly macabre ornament."

After uttering indecipherable words, the witch began twirling and crying as though kindled by an interior fire where evil and passion were fighting one against the other and the devil's touch was the prize. All the others joined in and a terrifying cacophony blast Becky's ears. Cries and heat were becoming more and more oppressive at the same pace.

Then Abigail looked deep into her eyes. "We all know that your attorney's ancestor was one of the bastards that condemned these girls for witchcraft, after searching their bodies for the devil's mark, of course."

She hadn't finished talking yet but the executed souls gathered before their guest, lowered their shawls and let their humiliated skeletons visible.

One stepped very close, "Our accuser's blood runs through your fiancé's veins, dear; don't you believe it's time to exact satisfaction?"

A flash of hellish light followed as though an evil spell had just been cast, only to be broken by the force of revenge. Becky felt the curse upon her.

Jason did share the judge's perversion. His means of seduction were more punitive than alluring and she often ended up in tears before his diverted glance. Was his morbid cruelty plain madness or something that went beyond even that?

"Drink this potion and your power will be granted," Abigail said, after pouring the content of a little bottle into a cup.

Becky swallowed it avidly. Victory was already in her heart.

She shuddered on seeing wrath and hate shape themselves in a grim shadow that literally stepped into her body and, with a wild cry, she fell to the floor. Immediately, the witches gathered around and dragged her by the fireplace.

The heat made the girl turn back to her senses. Was she going to be burnt too? Terrified, she burst into tears.

"Witches don't cry," said a sister dryly. "The spell didn't work."

"There must be something in the heart," remarked another, "some sort of feeling which is not compatible and works as an antidote."

Disappointed, they all gazed at Abigail who sentenced her, saying "She must leave at once."

Becky turned round for a last glance and was surprised to see that the cave had totally disappeared. Huge trees stood in its place, their branches swaying sinisterly in the impending nightfall.

The house now looked gloomier than ever; most certainly, it *was* a hiding place for those wretched girls whose spirits had moved to Abigail's cave... if it did exist, if Abigail existed...

She was still pondering the events when a familiar voice shouted, "Becky, open this damned door, it's freezing out here."

No sooner had Jason entered than he took her in his arms. "I hope you didn't feel too at home in this dreadful place."

"No reason I shouldn't," she replied coldly.

His presence upset her.

"Better get me a hot potion or I'll freeze to death, baby."

While sipping his coffee, he said in a most conceited tone, "I might even make it for the date, doll, but first you'll let me make sure you're not a witch," and with a raucous laughter, took out of his pocket a strange large pin.

An uncontrollable fury seized Becky; the turmoil of the witches' souls had become hers; before her eyes the flames of their stake, in her ears the inhuman cries of those who feel the first blazing embers on the flesh.

Had she turned into a real witch? Perhaps, the spell did work after all.

The knives in the block caught her glance, their blades emanating a lugubrious sheen... There was no time to waste; the urge of taking revenge empowered her with the spell of death.

She snatched the sharpest and plunged it into his heart.

A bewildered expression crossed Jason's face and his eyes opened in horror.

Much to Becky's astonishment, the deadly features slowly started changing and gained the aspect of an old man's one with hoary hair and a despicable grimace; the hideous judge for centuries buried in the attorney's body was lying at her feet, the pin tight in his hand.

Horrified, she stepped back without taking her eyes off the ghastly presence.

She was still incredulous when a hollow applause broke the silence. Abigail and her sisters had thronged into her house to express their contentment.

Little Dove

Donna L. Greenwood

Ever since she died, my daughter has been difficult to love. She doesn't feel right; she doesn't feel like Alice anymore. She smells different. She died three months ago and I wish she would die again – only this time, stay dead.

I try not to show her how I feel. I make her meals, I brush her hair, I let her sit with me when I tell her little brother bed time stories. When she catches me looking at her, she smiles, but I find it hard to smile back. Thank Heavens for Mikey, my little dove, four years old and bright as a pin, not tarnished like his sister.

'Mummy, you love Mikey more than me, don't you?' she asked me one day. What could I say? Yes, I do love him more because he doesn't stink of death? Because he didn't crawl from the grave after being three months dead and come knocking on the door?

I've tried to love her, but it's so very difficult. She creeps around the house, staring at Mikey with those large, empty eyes. Mikey doesn't say much but I think he's scared of her. I tell him, it okay, little dove, she's only a girl; what harm can she do?

***

It's her eyes. They were a bright green when she was born but death has darkened them to the colour

141

of graveside mud. In the night, I hear her chattering. The noises don't sound like words; they don't sound human. And sometimes, I hear other voices chattering with her but I know that she's alone. I cover my ears. I don't go and check on her.

***

Last night I caught her in Mikey's room, just staring at him lying in bed. She had this look on her face. I think he's better off sleeping with me, just for a little while.

***

People talk about priests in situations like this, but I don't know any. I don't go to church. I don't believe in God, but perhaps it's only God that can help us now. This morning she pushed me down the stairs. I had Mikey in my arms. I think she was trying to grab him and I lost my footing. Mikey's fine – a little bruised, as am I – but we're okay. For now.

***

Alice? I open the door. The room is cloaked in darkness. As I walk forward, I see my breath hanging in the air like a phantom. Her room is freezing. *Alice?* I whisper. I squeeze my eyes tighter in an attempt to see more clearly. I can just about see the shape of her. She's sitting on the floor, facing her wall. *Are you okay, honey?* I move a

142

little closer and then stop. For a moment I am paralysed, my breath and bones melt into a hot nothing and I can't move. Alice's head is turning without her body following. Her black eyes stare into mine. There are shadows moving around her, stroking her arms and kissing her face. She stands, her backwards head flops to the side and she points her finger at me. I am accused. Her upside -down mouth opens and she whispers one word – 'Mickey'.

***

I stroke Mikey's face as he sleeps on my lap. I've barricaded us into my room by pushing the dresser in front of the door. I've rung the police, the fire brigade and the ambulance but I'm frightened they will arrive too late. I can hear her walking up and down the corridor outside my room, whispering to herself. After a while, she knocks on the door. I wait, holding Mikey close. The silence screams for a moment, then there's a loud crash as the dresser thunders across the room. It ruches the carpet and falls over. The door opens and a skeletal hand crawls through the gap. It's her. She's coming for me. She pulls the rest of her body through the doorway. I watch her walk towards me and pull my little dove even closer..

'Please', I say, 'Please take me, but leave your brother alone.' She seems taller and her head is on the right way around. She holds out her long, spindly arms, more bone than skin.

'I won't let you hurt him,' I yell at her, 'You'll have to kill me first before you hurt him.'

She stares at me, her eyes black and empty.

'Mummy,' she says, 'Look,' And then she looks down at Mikey.

But I don't want to look at Mikey. I don't want to see.

'Look' she says again and this time I follow her gaze and look at my little dove, resting on my lap. Four years old and bright as a pin, my little Mikey. His face looks the same. I can tell it's my little boy but the skin has begun to putrefy. His eyes have gone, only bony sockets remain. Dead. My little dove is dead. He died with his sister three months ago - carbon monoxide poisoning.

I buried them both. I remember now. I buried them both, but I couldn't leave my little dove to sleep under the cold ground. He is so afraid of the dark. The earth had been remarkably easy to break open and the coffin was small and cheap. My son was soon back home with me.

Alice is still holding out her arms. This time when she smiles, there is kindness there.

'Mummy, let him go,' she says. And I do. I let him go.

I watch him rise from the shell that used to be him and I watch his sister take his hand. The two of them turn around and smile at me, Alice nods and whispers thank you and suddenly there is light and warmth in the room and I feel something soft brush against my face, like the soft wings of a dove finally set free.

To Run Is To Fly

Rie Sheridan Rose

The air was alive with wings. Red, blue, yellow, green... cascading, swooping, diving, soaring. And song—always song. Teeth fairly rattled with the trilling, cawing, cooing cacophony of it.

By contrast, the streets seemed dead. Gray buildings populated by gray people living gray lives. On occasion, a careworn face would turn toward the living rainbow above and an expression of wistful longing would lighten the gray to ash.

And sometimes, one of the birds would light on a bent shoulder and sing its song directly into a thirsty ear—an earthly benediction—before soaring off again... perhaps leaving a brilliant feather to be treasured like gold.

The gray folk stumbled and limped. Some held canes or crutches. No one ran.

Running was for the birds.

Here and there among the gray folk was a child—but these too were limping gray... or too young to run. Babes in arms were scattered about, toddling tots... toddled, but no one ran.

It wasn't forbidden. It was impossible.

Marta clung to her son. Talman was almost three. His golden hair was a spot of earthbound color in the gray town. His limbs were long and straight. He was a boy meant to run.

So she kept him close. Kept him pent. Tied his wrist to hers with string. Bound him to her shattered gait.

Talman watched the birds. Daily from barred windows he watched. He reached for them with straining fingers. Tears streamed down ashen cheeks as he watched the birds... and Marta watched him.

On the square, writ in stone, was the law: TO RUN IS TO FLY.

It was a curse long suffered.

No one remembered why it was cast—why they were doomed to gray ash. Even the eldest were born beneath its pall....

But the mothers like Marta held their babes close and prayed for twisted limbs. Hoping against hope.

To run was to fly.

One gray day, in a gray month of that gray year, as Marta fussed among her cooking pots, a glass was dropped, a string was cut and the tether anchoring Talman's straight limbs and dancing feet snapped in twain. Before the cry of horror could fully form on her ashen lips, he bolted out the open door into the winter-dark sunlight.

He hit the doorway running—at long last, running.

The change began on outstretched arms and upturned face. A shimmer of golden down, pin feathers, pinions, wings—soaring free by the time he reached the square. Golden bird from tow-haired child.

To run was to fly.

Above the Ceiling

Dan Allen

You turn the page on the same novel you've been reading since Christmas and your persistent cat jumps on your lap.

She growls.

That's something you've never heard her do and you lose your place. Her claws dig into your leg and she's fixed on the window. The blinds are closed, but her hearing is better than yours and you give up trying to read. You close your book.

"What's up, Nickie? You hear something?"

She growls, lower, only loud enough for you and pushes off your thigh. She crouches to the floor, tail down and stiff, eyes not leaving the window. You sense her fear and hold your breath, silencing the gravel rumbling in your chest and try to listen.

A bump. Something touched against the house. You turn in your chair to join Nikita in her stakeout.

Louder now, a sound of something slashing off the outside wall, perhaps claws dragging on the siding. You manage to move to the window and reach to open the curtains. A thump from the other side of the wall and Nikita looks at you like she's pleading *don't open the blinds, you old fool.* The cord is in your hand, all you need to do is pull down and see for yourself and you hesitate. The cat apparently decides to sit this one out and disappears under the bed.

"Some guard cat you are."

Best wait for Rosie, you think and return to your chair. You close your eyes and your thoughts drift to her sweet tobacco breath, whispering in your ear and large, meaty hands pulling you tight to her bosom. She talks like the truck driver she is and hasn't changed a bit since you married her. And then there's that other stuff, mean and hateful, but you don't want to think about that.

Footsteps, heavy and aggressive, cross right above where you sit—no attempt to be discreet, no soft, slow movement or tippy-toeing. You tilt your head and stare at the ceiling.

"Somebody's on the roof," you say into the empty room, so calm and matter-of-fact. You look to see if the cat will crawl from her sanctuary and help you confirm it. She never shows herself when afraid and maybe that's confirmation enough. There is a danger. It hangs in the air like static electricity, ready to spark and bite. A weapon? Yes, a weapon is something you need right now. Protecting your home is important and you think of an option.

You dig through the closet, pushing aside hanging pants and plastic dry-cleaning bags filled with dresses that haven't seen the light of day in decades. You drop to your knees and climb over a mountain of shoes, looking for your shotgun. It should be here, behind the clothes, leaning in the corner. You stop and try to remember; *did I ever have a shotgun?* You curse growing old and you curse your failing memory. In this house where you and Rosie live, there are no firearms and no weapons unless you count some old hockey sticks in the garage.

148

Hockey sticks. You remember hockey sticks. Back in the day, you could carve someone up good with the blade of a stick and you reward the memory with a smile. You could look in the garage, but the door's sealed. Rosie locks it from both sides so that nobody can get in and nobody can get out. She says she doesn't want you wandering away. That's crazy. People who live on the same street all their lives aren't going to forget where their house is. Rosie isn't reasonable and you wait for the opportunity to prove you can still handle being outside on your own.

You hear rattling and the deadbolt sliding. Somebody opened the front door and now they're in the house. You hear keys clank on the counter and a smoker's cough.

"Rosie? Is that you?"

"Who the hell do you think it is?"

You thought it was her, but you had to call out just in case. You remember Rosie, she talks tough, but she takes care of you and that's good enough.

"Did you lock the door?"

"Yes, I locked the damn door. Get your skinny ass to the table. I brought home some chicken."

She takes the last drag off her smoke and stubs it out amongst dead butts in an overflowing cloverleaf ashtray. You smile and recall stealing it from the bowling alley when you were first dating. Rosie hid it in her purse.

"Funny, what I remember."

"What's that?"

"Oh, shit. Something happened today, Rosie. You need to hear this." You tug on her hand and lead her to the front room.

"This better be good. I ain't had my supper yet." Rosie moves slow, exercise isn't in her daily schedule and her belly rolls from side to side. You're patient.

"There's somebody on the roof."

"You shittin' me? You pull me away from dinner for nuttin' and I might pop you one in the chops."

You hold a finger to your lips and shift on restless legs, urging her to stay quiet for a minute and listen.

"There ain't nobody on the damn roof, Dale. I bet you heard some squirrels."

"No, no, it wasn't squirrels. I heard big heavy footsteps, like a man." You fidget with your hands, rolling them over the top of each other. Nikita circles your legs and rubs against you. She sits on your feet and meows at Rosie as if to show her support for your testimony.

A sound, quick, scurrying…

"There. Did you hear that?" Your finger traces a line across the ceiling.

"Sure, sure, Dale. I hear Santy Clause." Rosie's sarcasm cuts you like a broken liquor bottle. Her attention, like her patience, all but gone.

"Come on, Rosie. Stop and listen for a minute."

"Maybe you heard some mice, Dale. Or maybe some squirrels. I don't know and I don't give a rat's ass."

Another noise, thumping.

"There, right there. Did you hear that?"

Rosie snorts, shakes her head and leaves you looking at the ceiling.

***

What was that? You ask yourself, but you're asleep and forgotten about the critter. You want to wake up, but you're deep at the bottom of the ocean and therE's so much swimming to do and you can't move your arms. You must. There's danger nearby. You fight through the paralysis and stir into consciousness.

There's something in the room. Where? Is it at the end of the bed, crouching low so it can't be seen? Your eyes are blurry and sleep has dulled your senses. You slap at the lamp, struggling to find the switch, but the room's too dark and you can't see. You pat the surface of your bedside table for your glasses. A fingertip nudges plastic and they fall on the floor, landing partway under the bed. *Forget the glasses. Who knows what's hiding under there?*

Scratching. Claws dragging on the plaster ceiling right above your head.

You sit up and listen. The critter is moving around, gnawing and chewing on something. How distressing. Noises in the walls, noises in the ceiling, animals, vermin perhaps intruding in your home.

"Rosie, Rosie, wake up." You gently push on her beefy shoulder.

She grunts and rolls to face you. One eye opens and you watch her pupil focus.

151

"Whaddaya want, shithead?" she says, not really upset, not yet. But she will be. Now that she's awake, she'll take her anger out on somebody.

"The attic," you say and you both remain perfectly still and wait.

"Squirrels?" asks Rosie.

"No, bigger than that."

"I don't hear it." She rolls back on her side. "You're an asshole, Dale. Go to sleep."

You stay awake for a minute, but sleep comes and you drift off.

***

The eastern sky is still dark and something moves around. Clunking sounds wake you and you squeeze Rosie's arm. You hear the noise again coming from the corner above and you stand on the bed and pound the ceiling. Dread and frustration pour out with each strike. Fear of what's in the attic and, of course, Rosie. *Why is Rosie to be feared? When did that start?* You don't know, but you know it's true.

"Get the hell out!" Angry, resolved and defiant.

Rosie moans and rolls over.

The scuffling stops, at least for a few seconds. Silence, a bizarre standoff until Rosie coughs, breaking the peace treaty and the ruckus continues. Three loud thumps followed by a long nails-on-a-chalkboard scrape.

"Don't think I liked the sounds of that," you say.

Scratching, digging, faster and faster.

Rosie sits up, her red hair tangled in a mess. "What the hell are you doing, Dale?"

You drop to your knees beside her, looking for an ally, maybe even comfort. "The fucker is trying to get in!"

She grabs you by your pyjama collar and pulls you in close. She's sweaty and a slip of night drool hangs from her lip. "I want you out of my house. You hear me? First thing in the morning I'm taking you to a home. You can be somebody else's problem."

***

When morning comes, Rosie is late and gets dressed without bothering you. Apparently, she has no intention of following through on her threat, at least not for now. The bedroom reeks of cigarette butts and spilt beer. You hear the keys rattle and the deadbolt move. After the door slams, the key turns again and the deadbolt engages. Rosie probably thinks you're oblivious, but you know she locks you in. Even on your bad days when you can't find your words and don't remember the cat's name, you feel isolated and know you're trapped.

You stay in bed and listen to the noises, a critter running back and forth exploring the boundaries of the attic. You know what it is. You can see it in your mind, the furry striped tail, the sharp black claws, the ringed eyes. What's its name? It's right there, right on the cusp of your memory. You squeeze your temples and it comes to you, flooding in on a wave of sunbeams and trumpets.

"Raccoon!" You shout, throwing up your arms as if you scored the winning goal. You'll tell Rosie. *She'll be pleased.*

***

Rosie will be home soon and you don't want to upset her. You hear her keys in the door and you wait for her in the kitchen.

"Rosie, I know what it is. I know it. It's a..." And the word leaves you. You look about the room and breathe too fast. Rosie is watching you and you know you only have seconds. You concentrate and see the beady little eyes behind the bandit's mask. "Raccoon."

You flash her your reward-winning grin, the one she giggled over when you were first married, but she throws her coat on the floor and lights a smoke.

"So, what did you do all day?" she asks, not interested in a raccoon and not interested in you either.

Think, you say to yourself, but you can't remember and you look at her with lifeless eyes and your mouth droops.

"Christ, Dale." She stomps out her half-smoked cigarette and points her finger. "Did you piss yourself?"

You are naked except for your pee-stained white cotton briefs. *I'm not dressed,* you think to yourself, confused about how this could be.

Nikita looks up at you and you imagine she can talk.

Why is she so mean?

"I don't know," You say out loud.

Later, the attic is quiet, and your sleep is undisturbed, except for Rosie's snoring.

***

You fill up the electric kettle in the morning and place it on the stove, turning the burner to high. In the bathroom, you swallow the day's blister pack of pills, measured out for you by the pharmacy. You remember preparing your own medications and wonder when that changed. Scurrying claws scrape above you and get your attention.

"The little fucker's back," you announce to the empty room and listen to the coon attacking the ceiling, its sharp claws dragging over the plaster, scratching and digging. You decide to fight the critter with noise and turn the television to full volume. A rambunctious studio audience screams and cheers at fools who choose to expose each other's dirty laundry. On the way back, you grab the broom. Nikita crouches low and slinks down the hallway, perhaps concerned over your intentions.

"Let's see if it likes this," you yell to her, hoping to be heard over the chanting from the show, calling for a fight and you punch the ceiling with the broom handle. You dance and hop around like a mischievous child. Poking and pounding, egged on by the television audience. They are cheering for you and you hammer away until a commercial break ends the hysteria.

The ceiling explodes. Small bits of plaster and insulation drop through a saucer-sized hole, creating a momentary diversion. A clawed paw pushes out and takes a wild swipe at the broom. You instinctively duck and raise your arms in a defensive motion.

"Piss off," you scream. Caught off guard, like a jump-out-of-your-seat scene in a thriller movie, you stiffen, trembling, too terrified to move. The critter is screaming too and pushes out more insulation. Its arm swoops down and claws come too close.

Two steps and you're in the hallway, closing the door behind. *I wonder how long this will hold?*

Nikita looks at you, annoyed as if you disturbed her nap. "What are you yelling for?" you hear her ask.

"Big raccoon, long blue arms and black claws. But no worries, I've got it trapped in the bathroom."

"You sure you're not worried, Dale?" asks the cat. "I heard you screaming like a baby and that door is hollow, you know. It's only a paper-thin veneer covering. I could claw through it myself."

You laugh at the cat and you're confident now with the bathroom door closed, but something tugs away at your brain. Something terrifying. Before you can work it out, you smell the toxic stink of melting plastic and see curls of smoke sneaking from the kitchen. The show comes back on and the crowd chants the host's name. You shut the TV off.

The kettle is destroyed, the bottom melted and warped. You hide it under the counter, saving yourself a beating. The house smells worse than an oil refinery and that's another problem. Nikita curls

156

on your lap and you fall asleep waiting for Rosie to come home.

***

"What the hell have you done now?" Her voice rumbles like rolling thunder and you're awake. You can't remember her name. You want to ask about her day, calm her down a little, but you are stuck. "Welcome home… Honey," you blurt out.

"Don't honey me. Why'd you mess up the bathroom?"

You stand, unable to answer, unable to recall. Rosie's hand catches you above an ear and you stumble, landing on your knees. The cat shakes her head and retreats behind the couch, turning her back on you.

***

Half asleep in the late evening hours, you open the bathroom door a crack and check if anything is on the floor, ready to charge. A glance at the ceiling makes sure the opening isn't any larger. You sit on the potty, trying to relax enough for the job at hand and your eyes never leave the hole. It's bigger now, you're sure, and your imagination tells you the plaster is moving, bulging ever so slightly. You give up and let relief wait until morning. Rosie follows you in and you wonder if you remembered to tell her about the raccoon. You sit on the toilet and watch her get ready for bed. Already in pyjamas, she finishes with her toothbrush and pulls out a jar.

An arm slides through the ceiling hole and three long fingers uncurl. You waste valuable seconds dumbfounded over a creature with three fingers and you watch the arm, hairless and dark blue, search around the ceiling. Each finger is capped with an oversized black claw, viciously hooked and scarred from use. The arm turns as if on hundreds of hinges and stretches further into the bathroom. It's scrawny and swings around, looking for something.

Rosie stands over the sink putting on her night face and you see her look into the mirror. The creature's blue arm hovers slightly beyond her shoulder and you watch the expression on her face change. She freezes, one hand covered in moisturizer and the other holding the jar. "Dale... Stop looking at me." She doesn't see it, not yet.

You stand, your pants around your ankles and struggle to pull them up. The blue arm swings, long knobby fingers spread like a three-digit peace sign and on the tip of each finger, slightly below the hooked claw, small slits emerge. They crack open only a smidgeon but enough for you to see the eyeballs. A single finger curls and touches the tip of your nose. It pokes at the bulbous end with the curiosity of a child. The eyeball opens and it pauses as if deciding your fate.

"Help me," you whisper and hold your breath.

Seconds later, the arm snaps back into the ceiling like a measuring tape retracting into its case. Dozens of small yellow eyes peer down at you from the hole in the plaster. Each one bobs and floats independently of the others. Although it can't be seen, there is a mouth. You can hear slobbering and smell rotten breath. Spittle drips out of the darkness and three drops land on your wrist, sizzling and burning your skin. The cigarette-sized spots form a triangle pattern and you marvel over their perfect roundness. You saw the acid drip, yet your mind flashes back to a recent memory of your arm twisting and the smell of tobacco. *She burns me.*

The critter slides a shotgun down from the attic. That's where your guns are. You remember hiding them away decades ago. The pump-action feels good in your hands and you marvel at how pretty it looks. Rosie must see it, too, because the cream jar slips through her hand and she grabs the sink edge to keep herself from falling to the floor.

"Where the hell did you get the gun, Dale?"

You're afraid and hold it out to her. She jerks the weapon out of your hands and turns it on you. An explosion smacks you in the chest and lifts you off your feet, slamming you into the bathtub. You're not sure if she did it on purpose or if it was an accident. She doesn't panic and calmly leaves, perhaps to call for help. She returns with a short glass (a treasured souvenir from a trip to Boston) and pours herself three fingers of whiskey. She makes herself comfortable on the tub edge, takes a mouthful and wipes her lips with the back of her hand.

The front of your t-shirt is crimson and you feel no pain. A lake is forming beneath you and you imagine you're a boat. Your world grows dim and you decide there must be something wrong with the bathroom lights. Rosie takes out a menthol and lights it. Her zippo sports the Harley Davidson logo and you don't remember giving it to her a few years back. She watches you while she smokes and for once, she is patient and interested. You are happy for the attention, but your eyes are heavy and you slump, the side of your face resting in the sticky lake. Sleeping on her would be rude and Rosie surely would be angry, so you struggle to stay awake.

You wonder if everything is in slow motion. Danger approaches Rosie and you watch from only feet away and from miles at the same time. Blinded by a white flash, you wait as the world comes back into focus and everything looks like the reversed image of an x-ray. You recognize an electrical smell and the word ozone forms in your mind.

A disgusting mangy beast crawls on the ceiling. Clumps of blue are missing and you wonder if monsters shed their fur. There is no definitive head or abdomen, only a bulging, twitching mass with multiple arms protruding at seemingly random angles, completely ignoring any natural symmetry. Each coiling arm ends with three fingers and each finger with a claw and an eye.

The furry spider-like blob lowers itself behind Rosie and blue arms loop around her neck, the claws sinking in under her jaw bone. Her smoldering cigarette falls from her lips, embers spark off the porcelain and turn to ash. The critter lifts her in the air, smashes her into the plaster and twists her neck with a quick snap. Her head bends at an impossible angle and her face is purple. One lifeless eyeball bulges too far from its socket and the tip of her tongue sticks out between her lips. The whiskey bottle slides through her fingers and smashes.

A blue arm extends down and fingertip eyes watch you. You open your mouth to speak, but only salty liquid gurgles from your lips. Your eyes close and you think of your mother. You hear the critter say, "Be Free." In your mind, you see your front door fall off its hinges and voices, thousands of them, welcome you from your isolation. You drift across the threshold and the events of your lifetime pour back into your grasp. You remember.

Dreams of Duality

Dorothy Davies

Gordon Lansard sleeps. He sleeps and his dreams are tortured and tormented: they run wild with blood and body parts, they are dark and dangerous and he wakes sweating, crying aloud with the horror of all he has seen and thinks he has done. He reaches for the person at his side, cries when he remembers she is not there. And cries again when he remembers why she is not there.

Gordon staggers from his bed and heads for the bathroom on autopilot, visions of the darkness still clouding his mind and his thoughts. He stares into the mirror on the cabinet, wondering why someone who looks so normal, so much the average businessman earning a living by shuffling papers and ticking boxes, should dream of prowling the streets in a form inhuman and inhumane in every way.

Last night's dream had been particularly bad. Even as the razor touches his skin and disturbs the foam he has applied to the more-than-average face, he recalls the gushing foam that spouted from 'his' mouth, foam that burned and choked and ate into flesh like acid. Who and what could devise such a creature, such a monster, and implant it in his dreams? The biggest question was - why?

He showers, hoping the water will cleanse and revitalize him. Another day is ahead, another day of polite talk and inane inter-office chatter, of bad coffee and worse restaurant food.

Of an attempt to numb his mind before he goes to the psychiatrist to talk about the dreams.

***

"Last night's was the worst yet." He hates lying on the couch with the man sitting so cosily by his head, notebook in hand, scribbling things he cannot see and probably would not understand if he could, hates being there relating the nightmares. It sounds so much as if he is going off his head and he knows he isn't, knows he is perfectly sane - apart from the dreams. And they were only dreams, after all. "I was all but screaming when I woke from it."

"Tell me." The voice is professionally smooth, professionally caring but he could be calculating how much he has earned that day for all the genuine emotion coming through. Gordon sighs and allows himself to remember. This is always the worst part, he part he dreads more than any other. He would prefer to forget each dream on waking but he knows they are getting worse and he needs to sort them out. If he can. If anyone can.

"It was a full moon. Now, before you say were-wolf, no, it wasn't, I wasn't. The full moon helped me/it see better, it didn't influence the creature. We were in the – this sounds snobbish, I know – the cheaper side of town, where the estates are litter strewn and no streetlights shine, all been smashed out of existence, like the people who live there. I did say it sounded snobbish. I'm telling you because

163

it's the truth and because you can't tell anyone else, right?

"Right." No condemnation in the voice whatsoever. No emotion in the voice whatsoever, Gordon noted. What did he have to do to get this man to display humanity of some kind?

"I was – I have to say I, it gets tedious otherwise, I was running through the streets, not fast, fast enough that I could go from one really dark shadow to the next without being seen, but not so fast that I couldn't miss a single scent. I saw him on the corner of the street, the junction of two main roads. He was scanning the buildings, no doubt looking for one to break into. He had tools of some kind in his hands and pockets. I don't know how I knew this but I did. He didn't hear me coming, he didn't get a chance to scream or even gasp. I had him by the back of the neck on the ground in an instant; I tore his head off in the next instant and let it roll into the gutter. I drank the blood which gushed out. I tore at the flesh and consumed as much of it as I could before I felt the ground vibrate and knew someone or something was coming that way. If it was a car, I had to get out of sight fast. If it was a person, I didn't want a second kill but I didn't want to be seen, either. I left the body there and ran. This time I did run fast, down dark alleys and round the back of garages, hiding where I could. I recall it was surprisingly easy to hide, considering I was a very large animal indeed. Larger than a man would be on all fours, much larger. Almost lion size but without the lion's huge mane. And smooth. Very, very smooth. No hair.

164

None at all. Nothing to snag on wire or fencing, nothing to catch on brick or stone. The taste of flesh was good. The taste of blood was better. I ran and ran until I had no more energy and then - I woke."

"Interesting."

Gordon stares at the ceiling, noticing for the first time that it was patterned. He knew the walls well, the calm pale green paint, the deeper green curtains, the tastefully framed professional certificates, the expensive looking landscape behind the desk. But the ceiling, surely that was new. The pattern was random and looked like-

"You are relating the dreams in more detail, Mr. Lansard." The sound of pages being turned distracts Gordon from his assessment of the ceiling for a moment. "When you first came your dreams, as related by you, were of killing and eating but not in such detail, not where you were and who you killed. It is as if some hatred is eating away at you and is manifesting itself in the dreams. Do you hate your work and co-workers that much is one question I have to ask of you?"

"Do I hate them… no, I'm totally indifferent to them. They talk, they smile, they're friendly but we're not friends. I'm known as the loner, they accept that."

"That's on the surface, Mr. Lansard. I need you to look deeper than that. Perhaps next time you come we can delve a little further into that part of your life. Meantime, perhaps we could go back to your childhood…"

When Gordon left, ¾ hour later, he wonders why he bothers to go. No answer to the cause of the dreams, no clue as to why the dreams were so horrific they leave him wanting to scream, exhausted and ill. But was there anywhere else to go? Anyone else to confide in?

Over a beer in the nearby pub he broods on the childhood questions the man would want to discuss. Nothing he could think of. Perfectly normal childhood, one brother serving overseas in the Army, parents alive, elderly but alive, a few cousins who used to come and play but who now had their own lives and himself...

Lonely and lost without his wife and still mourning the child they would have had.

None of that would account for nightly dreams of blood and mayhem.

They were dreams, for there was nothing in the paper or on TV about a serial killer on the loose, a dangerous animal tearing people to pieces. The police would not be able to keep that quiet. Therefore, it wasn't happening in real life but God, the dreams were real!

He bought herbal sleeping pills before going home, in the vague hope they would help him have a dreamless night.

They didn't.

***

"You look a bit peaky this morning, Gordon, old chap." The office gossip, Brewster, Vrooster, something like that anyway, was in front of his desk. "Overdid the booze last night, did you?"

"No, took some sleeping pills, actually. Not been sleeping too well lately."

Truth never came amiss, saves remembering the lies later.

"Brooding too much about work, I bet. Leave it here when you go home, old chap, it isn't worth taking home with you."

"You're right."

Gordon reached for a file, opened it and stared at the blood splattered sheet which presented itself to his eyes. Where had that come from? He closed the cover before anyone could see it, then examined his hand, his arm, his face. Dry. Not a wound to be felt or seen.

He opened the file again. The paper was pristine white, not so much as a mark or smudge.

He closed his eyes and counted to ten. The paper was still white when he looked at it.

Were the dreams intruding on his real life? If so, he had best get to a proper doctor soon, not the trickster who called himself a psychiatrist and who had nothing to offer but questions he did not want to answer.

With a sigh he began work, hoping to dull his mind, as always, to his night life.

***

The streets were dark, deserted, foggy. No sound, not even a distant engine or train rattling down worn silver rails on its way to nowhere and back again. He stood with his back to a partly demolished building, sensing the breeze coursing through the

167

glass-less window frame. He wondered for a moment why he didn't think pane-less rather than glass-less, then realized the word pane was also said as pain and he had enough of that surging through his body. It was as if his blood was on fire and burning every nerve end he had. He most certainly was not pain-less. This was new. This was unwelcome. This was crippling in a way. If he hurt he could not run. Or could he?

He pushed himself away from the building and began to trot along the empty cold pavements, avoiding the broken slabs, the potholes, the glass which appeared to be everywhere. His pads did not need glass shards in them.

As he trotted he found himself chanting a mantra:

I am not a werewolf. I am not a werewolf. I am a –

And there it stopped. Each time he reached the *I am a-* it turned back to *I am not a werewolf.* His mind refused to say what he was.

The trot became a flat out run and the pain eased; nerve endings coated with vast amounts of adrenaline or something. The fire was being put out but the hunger wasn't. The need to eat was all-consuming, *excuse the pun* he thought and smiled, realising his face twice the size it normally was, his mouth three times larger than his human one and containing far more teeth. The next question he asked, as he saw a lone human walking, hurrying along the cold walkway of a block of flats, was why this non-human aspect wasn't bothering him at all.

168

The walkway was dark, darker than the street, perfect for an ambush. The human, a woman, did not hear him coming. Her blood was sweet and her flesh was sweeter.

***

Gordon Lansard woke in a bed of tumbled twisted sheets and duvet, pillows thrown on the floor, mattress half skewed off the base of the bed. He sat up, groaning at the heaviness in his head and body. He felt many times his normal weight, everything was difficult. It required a super-human effort on his part to actually stand, walk, get to the bathroom, where he saw his normal self in the mirror, dark rings under his eyes, grime – or was it dried blood? – under his fingernails. A long hot shower took care of the grime, if that is what it was, but the dark rings remained. He looked like a man who had not slept properly for a week.

On a whim he stepped on the bathroom scales. They registered a weight loss that shocked him. He had been a big man, now he was becoming a shadow of himself. The doctor would be checking for cancer if he went to see him, but he had no pain – in this life, he told himself and wondered why – and also realized he was not eating – in this life.

There was the oddity again. Not in this life. In what life did he have pain, then and in what life did he eat?

The answer, which had been staring at him from the mirror for some time, shocked him more than his weight loss.

169

The dreams were real.

How did he know this? He couldn't say; it was as if a light had come on in his darkened mind. It was the only thing which made sense, of the dreams, of the reality that was his body in this time.

In his dreams he travelled to – what? A parallel world, an alternate reality? In that other world he was – a monster. A travesty of a human. One that killed without compunction, just so he could live. Because none saw him, none could stop him. But what could stop him? Silver bullets were for werewolves which were mythical anyway. Again, were they? Did werewolves exist in the alternate world he walked in night after night? Was his life here of no consequence at all, was that the only reality for him? Would he go to sleep one night and not wake up again in this life?

Questions he could not answer. Questions he doubted anyone could answer. Such things were best kept between the pages of horror novels or in scripts for horror films, not for a suburban businessman, widower, son and brother as he was.

It was as if the very essence of him evaporated in that moment and he sat on the toilet seat, drained of emotion and, had he been able to see in the mirror, of blood.

Widower.

His beloved Eloise had died in a horrific incident covered up by the police, consigned to the darkest drawer in the archives.

She had died when 'something' had attacked her, ripped off her head and consumed most of her flesh; including the unborn child she carried. It had been a closed coffin funeral.

Gordon struggled to the telephone and called in sick.

He dressed, with an effort, before he could change his mind. He left the house, locking it securely behind him. He set off for the town, walking because he did not trust himself behind the wheel of the car. Who knew what damage he could do in his current state of mind?

He walked until he saw the spire of the local parish church looming above the roofs of the houses surrounding it. It had to be a church; everything said it had to be holy, to offset that which he had become. He prayed, earnestly, that it would be open. So many churches were locked because of vandalism, because of vagrants and because of thieves. He could be all or any of those things but for once he needed the sanctuary of the church.

It was open. The great ancient door creaked as he pushed against it and then closed it behind him, hearing the iron latch drop into place. The sun threw colours into the aisle for him to walk on. They hurt his feet as he stepped through them and he wondered why. Then he realized his shoes hurt, that his pads wanted to feel the carved tombstones which made up the aisle. He did not give way to the impulse.

Before the altar was a wooden rail and hassocks for him to kneel down. He stared at the sacred cross, sacred because of two thousand years of worship of it as an icon, a symbol of all that was good. He prayed for salvation, for a cure, for the dreadful evil that lived within him and appeared every night to send him on a journey which ended in death and destruction, to be taken from him. He prayed for something good to take its place.

He prayed throughout the whole day without breaking off for anything, no food, no water, no bathroom breaks.

When the sun began to leave the sky and the colours faded from the aisle, he got to his feet, stiff and aching – and empty.

Gordon Lansard looked up at the huge figure of Christ carved in the rood screen and yelled one word:

HALLELUJAH!!!

before leaving the church.

That night he dreamed an angel with a flaming sword was standing at the foot of his bed, calling him to go into another parallel universe.

Lost and Damned

Olivia Arieti

The tavern wasn't exactly a den of thieves, but its reputation was rather dubious and the clients even more. It was called 'The Devil's Den' as the shadiest fellows dropped in for the most promiscuous affairs. The guys were totally depraved and the girls behaved more like witches than fairies; vanity was their strength, jealousy their fuel. Drinking and gambling were the men's favourite pastimes, while selling their beauty was the ladies' one. They were all good friends, their common inclination to vice bound them in a perverse but solid complicity.

Nothing diverted them more than the few strangers who occasionally stopped by. Induced to drink heavily and enticed by the most seductive arts, the poor chaps were easily deceived and in an instant would lose a life's fortune on a game of dice before being thrown out among the sneers of the triumphant gamblers and the giggles of the diverted wenches.

As soon as Leonard entered and sat at a remote table in one of the darkest corners, the company's rapacious eyes began scrutinising him; his haughty demeanour and the elegant though outdated attire couldn't go unnoticed.

"We're going to have fun tonight," sneered Dan, "bet the bloke's pockets are full of dough."

"Truly appealing," whispered Scarlet to Lucille, already kindled by the fire of competition.

"The guy looks lonely," Joe remarked, "let's move over to his table."

The company hurried towards their victim and, like voracious vultures, plummeted before him.

"Drinking alone is never a good idea, Sir," said Dan.

Leonard first gazed at him, then slowly let his glance fall upon the others; a sinister flash crossed his eyes and his mouth attempted a sly smile.

"Most true, let me offer you and your friends here a drink," and slightly nodded to the barman.

By now the satanic light of the eyes was evident and, although an old-fashioned gallantness tempered his ways, his presence was disturbing. To add to it, the black cloak and gloves recalled a most disquieting character that had just come out of the set of a horror film or stepped down from the stage of an atrocious tragedy. The perversity that transpired from his person though was cunningly masked by a wicked charm that mitigated the company's uneasiness and awe.

The drinks were strong, much stronger than the ones they usually drained without a flinch.

"You're new here, I reckon," uttered Scarlet seductively."Wouldn't mind showing you around."

"I'm sure our friend is on the lookout for some merriment and we are the best guys in town to make you have a damned bloody good time," said Joe.

"Always been around," the stranger replied firmly, before ordering other drinks.

The men had lost all hope of getting him down to gambling and the girls wondered if he was immune to desire when Leonard, unexpectedly put his hand on Lucille's.

"Better watch out, buddy, the doll's mine, but I might be willing to compromise for tonight," Dan sneered.

"No hurry, man," and the same sly smile brightened his face, apparently reddened by the light of the lanterns placed here and there.

"I was wondering if you'd like to come to my Masquerade Ball. We'll make big deals there," Leonard said and cast a lustful glance at the girl. "Nothing better than a masquerade to conceal and, why not? reveal our most vicious secrets or aspirations."

Lucille had to lower her eyes blurred by the intensity of the stranger's gaze, while an unusual heat inflamed her whole body as though she was burning at the stake.

"Great fun is granted as nothing is forbidden," Leonard promised before concluding with scorn, "If you dare to come, of course."

Without waiting for a reply, he got up abruptly and, with a swirl of his ample cape, walked out.

Naturally, the dissolute party couldn't ignore the provocation, not even when they learnt that the ball would take place in the most haunted spot in the area, a creepy villa in the outskirts renowned for being infested with terrifying supernatural creatures.

The following night, a witch, a gypsy, a vampire and a grim reaper stood on the threshold of the dreary house.

No sooner they had entered than they began feeling as uneasy as ever. A bleak guy who resembled the barman guided them through a long and narrow corridor lit by candles only and then down a steep staircase. Even though he assured them they were heading for the ballroom, the party felt as though they were descending into the deepest abyss.

The room was enormous with more than one fireplace; the flames swaying voraciously, appearing animated by an evil fierceness that made them a dominant presence in the obscure hall.

The heat was oppressive and Scarlet wondered why the heavy curtains hadn't been drawn and the windows opened.

Leonard, in a black damasked tailcoat and a red shirt with ruffles, was anxiously waiting for them.

"Here's our lord of the Underworld," whispered Joe nervously.

"Welcome to my home," their host said, "it's an honour for me to have such precious guests tonight," and with a hot hand clapped Dan's shoulder, "Damned souls are our favourites, aren't they?"

When Scarlet felt that same hand around her waist while twirling on the ballroom floor, she feared it would set her gown on fire.

"Your costume is lovely," Leonard whispered, "nothing more punishable than a wicked witch," and laughed raucously as a sardonic expression crossed his face; now much redder than at the tavern. It perfectly matched his shirt but at the same time, made a sharp contrast with the sable cloak he majestically swirled as he danced.

She soon noticed that his ears were slightly pointed, but only when Lucille was in his arms the horns, red claws and spiked tail became manifest.

"So you changed your costume," exclaimed Joe and added, "Can't deny this place looks like hell itself."

Their host's demoniac laughter followed as the flames literally stepped out of the fireplaces and began invading the whole room.

"That's where you all belong and where you'll keep on burning, forever my guests."

The blazing tongues grew higher as the devil's laughter grew louder.

The desperate souls had just enough time to realize they had been tricked by a creature far more crafty and evil than themselves.

The Lute Woman

Sheree Shatsky

The lute woman plants the children heads up in the field, packing the soil tight around the wee necks level to the dimpled chins. She stands back and admires her work. The tousled heads pop like a row of sweet cabbages. Not a loll or list in the bunch.

She sets out the smudge pots to ward off the wolves and takes guard. A silver teaspoon pitted with the bite marks of tiny resistant teeth clinks the laudanum tincture shoved deep in the pocket of her dirty house dress. With ease, she spirited the children away from warm feathered beds with songs from the old days, the playful delicate rich notes plucked from her lute tendriling off and away and into the village, reaching through open windows and tap-tap-tapping at the closed, the notes murmuring, *what do you want, what do you need, I have chocolates, come and see.*

The sun rises to Stonehenge streams of light between each head and there, she plunges a tiny pagan cross deep in the soil, blessing the earth, marking her rows for potatoes, rhubarb and beans. The church bells sound in the distance, a panicked clanging in discovery of empty beds and wads of muslin pulled from small ears singing of chocolate. She soon will join the villagers in search for the missing, in listen of whispered wicked rituals, of warnings to beware the phantom lute woman who hunts for children to plant in her field the night before the summer solstice. She faces the sun with outstretched arms, embracing the glow. *"Oh, great and powerful Sol, the warmth over my crops, I welcome you, oh bringer of life. Please accept these gifts."*

She draws back her scythe and tops the towhead first, chocolate smeared across his sweet cabbage cheeks.

Bobby Bumping

Diane Arrelle

Brett yawned, taking his hands off the steering wheel to stretch. At five-thirty in the morning he had no oncoming traffic to worry about. In fact, the only thing he was worrying about on this South Jersey back road was the occasional stray deer. He shuddered involuntarily and gripped the wheel again as he remembered how a deer had taken out the entire rear quarter panel of Tim's old Buick. If Bambi could do that to one of those gas guzzling tankers from the seventies, imagine what it could do to his tin and plastic import.

He straightened up and glanced at his watch. Working the night shift at the casino really screwed up his life, but the money was too good to complain. "So what if I don't have a social life?" he mumbled, stifling another yawn. "I'll get on the day shift soon. Just need to be patient."

Brett frowned as a fog seemed to roll in out of nowhere. One minute it was a clear night with daylight hiding just behind the eastern horizon and the next he was in cream of mushroom soup. He tried to concentrate on the road but he was so tired. He blinked, fighting the urge to close his eyes, to rest them just for a moment. He slowed, then picked up speed. *Better to get home faster than to be lost in this mess,* he thought. After all, he knew that when he felt this exhausted, the quicker he was safe in his own bed, the better off he'd be.

180

Suddenly there was a figure standing on the road in front of him. Brett practically stood on his brakes, but he knew it was a reaction way too late to do any good. He covered his eyes, but not before seeing the terror on the kid's face just before he heard that hideous thump-bump-crack. He was sure by the sound the teenager had bounced onto the hood and into his windshield.

Brett sat, his eyes covered, his foot still jammed on the brake and waited, hoping to hear a sound; a moan, a groan, a "hey buddy, watch where you're driving." But all he heard was the intolerable silence that made the slow motion time seem even slower.

After what felt like hours, Brett uncovered his eyes and shifted the car into park. The fog was lifting; he could see the smoky lake off to the left and the scrubby pines off to the right. He could hardly see anything straight ahead because the windshield glass was spider-webbed with cracks and a few streaks of red. "Oh no, no, no, no," he moaned, watching a red droplet roll down the glass, catch in a crack and fan out. "Oh, no, what have I done?"

He waited another minute, then two, hoping that something would happen, hoping that something would move, hoping the guy he just slammed into would get up and yell at him. Finally, he gave up hope and slowly undid his seatbelt. He gingerly opened the door and waited. He didn't know what he was waiting for, but nothing happened. He thought about all those horror movies from his adolescent years and a new fear started to gnaw at him. He wanted to get out, see if he could help the kid, but he sat frozen. *What if he's not dead, but undead instead*, Brett wondered, fighting off an urge to shut the door and drive away. *What if he's going to grab my ankles as soon as I step out of this car and drag me off to the lake? Nobody'd miss me till tonight. Tim wouldn't even know I'm gone until his next day off or until he didn't find my rent check on the table at the end of the month. What if I've wandered into a real life slasher flick?* Brett laughed, a little too loud for his liking and perhaps a little to shrill. "I'm getting hysterical!" He shook his head and told himself, "Time to be a man about this!"

He stepped out of the car, hesitated a second, waiting to be grabbed and dragged, then slowly inched toward the front of the car. He saw the feet first, then the twisted legs and he knew that the kid was beyond help. As the head came into view, bent at a wrong angle, Brett lost control and threw up. He held the crumpled fender for support or he was sure he would have collapsed; his knees were so rubbery. "What do I do?" he asked the kid when he straightened up. "What do I do?"

He wiped at his cheeks and found them wet. He touched his tears, amazed that he was crying. "Like a baby," he mumbled and realized that was exactly how he felt at that moment. Like a helpless baby waiting for Mommy or Daddy to come make everything better. But Mom and Dad were back in Washington and he was alone on a secondary road buried in the Pine Barrens between two hick towns in Cape May County. The town he was living in didn't even have a police department; they probably didn't even have 9-1-1 yet.

He walked backwards, unable to take his eyes off the body until it was blocked by the front end of his car. He slid back in and sat behind the wheel. After closing the door, he couldn't help but quickly glance at the backseat. Finding it clear of monsters and maniacs, he sighed then tried to figure out what to do.

He wished he had his cell phone on him, but he didn't.

What was he supposed to do, leave the scene of the accident and go look for a state trooper or stay here? He knew it was a crime to leave an accident but was he negligent to remain and wait for a passing car? He decided to stay. The kid was already dead and he was guilty of hitting him. The sky was pink and the stars had retreated so he knew someone would be along eventually. He locked the door and closed his eyes. He knew sleep was out of the question so he sat there resting his eyes. And wondered about his life.

Would he go to jail? He doubted it, but he could lose his license. If that happened he'd have to move back to Absecon Island and depend on Jitneys again. No, he couldn't do that either. The rents were just too high in Atlantic City.

Meeting Tim had been a really lucky break. They had started out working the same shift and before he knew it they had become friends. One evening over drinks and a pizza, Tim said, "You know I've got a big house about forty-five minutes from here and since Dad died, I'm living there alone. Why don't you rent from me? We're going on different shifts next month so the place will be yours all day and mine all night. I'll make the price right!"

Brett sipped his drink, did some quick figuring and decided that even with the added mileage and wear and tear on his car this was a deal he couldn't afford to pass up. Of course, he hadn't figured on this kind of wear and tear, but it had worked out until now. He and Tim got along and had no problems sharing, and it was nice to have a big old farm house to entertain in the few times he had brought someone back with him.

***

He hadn't heard the approaching car and jumped when he heard the knock on his window. He thought he was going to die on the spot, his heart was facing so fast. It was full daylight and he saw Tim standing by the side of his car.

"Hey, Brett? What's the matter? Why you sitting here? Break down?"

Brett blinked for a moment and gathered his jumbled thoughts. That knock on the window scared him just about as much as the accident. "Tim! Boy, am I glad to see you! Go get some help!"

"What's the matter?"

Brett frowned with exasperation. *What was wrong with Tim*? "Go get the cops, can't you see he's dead?"

Tim frowned back, "Who's dead?"

184

"The kid! What's the matter with you?"

Tim glanced around. "Nothing's the matter with me, what kid? Where?"

"The kid in the front of my car!" Brett yelled and pointed. He stopped and took in a quick breath. His windshield was intact, no cracks, no blood. Perfect.

He pushed the door open, knocking Tim to the side and rushed to the front of the car. The road was empty, no mangled body, no pool of blood. Only Brett's vomit on the side showed that anything had gone on at all. "I... I... hit a kid last night, killed him."

Tim nodded, "Don't worry about it, let's go get a coffee back in town and we'll talk. Can you drive?"

Brett felt confused by Tim's lack of reaction but followed him to the coffee shop. They ordered and as they sipped coffee, Tim asked, "Foggy last night?"

Brett nodded, the coffee turning bitter as new fear gnawed at his guts. He was sure he wasn't going to like anything Tim had to say.

"You hit a teenage boy about seventeen or so wearing an orange and blue windbreaker and a red Phillies cap?"

Brett nodded again, taking a sip of water to try to get the bad taste of horror out of his mouth.

Tim smiled, "Well, Brett, you wouldn't have believed me before, but the kid's Bobby Watson. He died about twenty years ago in a hit and run accident on that road. Happened on a foggy spring night. It was a terrible thing, the talk of the town for months. Guy who killed him was never found."

Brett sighed, "So, every foggy night the ghost of the poor kid searches the road looking for peace, right?"

Tim shrugged. "I know it sounds like a cliché, but he's been hit repeatedly for years, always dies the same way, broken neck after bouncing off the windshield."

Brett sat and played with the coffee cup, spilling brown liquid onto the tabletop. "I'd laugh, except it happened to me. I killed a ghost!"

Tim grinned. "You know it's sick, but it's kind of a sport out here. They call it Bobby Bumping. People sometimes go out on a foggy night looking to hit him, it's the ultimate thrill."

Brett shuddered, "Some thrill! That was the worst feeling in the world. I thought I had killed another person!"

Tim grinned, "Yeah I know, but after the first few times, it's sort of fun."

Brett stared at his friend, "You've gone in for that sport?"

Tim reddened, "Well... yeah... you know, at first you don't want to, then the next thing you know, you see the kid in front of you and you know he's only a ghost and that you can't hurt him and well... it just happens."

Brett felt a shiver run up his spine. It had been an awful feeling, but the adrenaline rush had been exciting and it was certainly safer than the rush you'd get from drugs or sky diving.

He shook those thoughts off. "I think I'm calling it a day. I need sleep. I'm just happy I didn't really hurt someone." He stood up to leave, shook his head and added, "Who'd ever believe that there really are ghosts? Really!"

***

A few nights later, Brett was driving home on the same road when the fog grew dense again. He knew that this was a common occurrence out here in the springtime when the temperatures change quickly near water but he slowed down to a crawl. He was on the lookout for poor Bobby Watson. Then, just as before, the kid was in front of him, terror frozen on his face. Brett hit the brakes and the car barely nudged the kid, yet Bobby flew onto the hood and smashed his face into the windshield.

Brett stared in amazement. He felt sickened, but not like last time. Now he understood. Whenever the kid appeared, he had to be hit. It was all obvious to him now. He didn't even get out this time; he just stopped until the shaking went away. He drew a deep breath and began to drive toward home. He waited for the crunch as he ran the kid over, but there was none. The minute he started forward, the cracked windshield cleared and everything was back to normal.

Brett grinned, despite the disgust he was feeling with himself. It was sort of fun in a morbid way. And he hadn't hurt anyone, in fact it was kind of his duty to hit the kid and send him back.

Before he realized it, Brett was the number one Bobby Bumper around. He never wanted to admit it, but he looked forward to the fog. *It's not like I go out and wait for the stuff*, he thought as the white mist started to rise off the road one morning. _It's just a fact of nature. He looked around and saw that it was going to be a thick one; it was usually thickest if it started right before the dawn light. Brett felt high, He accelerated, looking for the solitary figure waiting to be sent back to purgatory.

"There he is," Brett yelled like a cowboy at the rodeo and floored the gas pedal. The little car roared as it rushed toward impact. "Yeehaw!" Brett bellowed as the body flipped onto his car and smashed into his windshield. "Bullseye!"

Brett drove the rest of the way home, feeling satisfied, like he'd just won at the table or had the best sex ever. He glowed with triumph, flavored with a small dash of guilt and a pinch of disgust.

Once in the house and out of the glow, he felt a full dose of remorse and disgust. "This really is sick! I'm going to give it up."

He nodded to himself and decided that although the other route was a few minutes longer he wasn't going on the Bobby Road until the foggy season was over.

"I can be strong!" he said as he prepared for his day-lit night. "I don't need the thrills, I'm going to enjoy my life the way it should be lived. Maybe in a few months I'll move back to the island. I bet I can find a roommate to share an apartment."

He slept all day, satisfied that he was a strong-willed person. That night he took the long way to work and basked in his display of willpower. But as the night dwindled down to the wee hours and he clocked out and got into his car, he realized that he was hopelessly addicted to the sport. "I'm a weak piece of garbage!" he snarled. "Well, I'll do it just one more time. Yeah, just once more and then I swear I can give it up!"

Brett drove home on the Bobby Road. He felt disappointed when the sky remained crystal clear and there was no hint of a fog rising. Just as he gave up all hope of Bobby Bumping, a light mist began forming. Brett shouted and sped up. The mist thickened into a full sheet of sight-obscuring white and he drove even faster. If this really was the last time, it had to be the best.

The figure emerged, a dark blur in the fog. Brett gunned the engine and surged ahead. His little car had never gone so fast. He braced for the impact and wasn't disappointed at all. The figure smashed into the car and crashed into the windshield so hard the glass actually broke. Brett hit the brakes, reversed, then accelerated forward so the figure would slide off and under his wheels.

But this time something was different. Brett fought off a shudder as the body crunched under his tires and the car bumped up and down.

"That's not supposed to happen," he mumbled, an uncomfortable feeling trickling through his nerves.

He slowed down to barely a crawl but kept going and the trickling turned into a full buzz of fear when the windshield didn't fix itself.

The spiderwebbed glass remained broken and he started shaking. *What's wrong*, he wondered, fighting the panic that was threatening to close off his windpipe.

"I couldn't have possibly hit a real person," he reassured himself just as the fog suddenly lifted and the sky to the east grew light with the sunrise. "Who'd be out on the road at this hour anyway?"

He slowed even more when he saw the orange flashers blinking in distress right up ahead. He stopped dead after he passed Tim's Buick sitting on the side of the road with the hood up.

He started to cry when he saw in the new day's sunlight the small, crumpled, lump on the road reflected in his rearview mirror.

First Fruits

Chris Rodriguez

The guidebook described the Caesarea Philippi as the Grotto of Pan. Selene clucked her tongue and scoffed at the idea of a mythological creature that was half man, half goat. Being educated, she had heard of Pan, but she came on this tour of the Holy Lands because she was deeply religious and wanted to walk in the footsteps of Christ, so to speak.

She noticed some of the tourists chucked things like flowers and fruit into the mouth of the cave. The water that in ancient times flowed from the opening of the grotto had long ago been diverted. Even if Pan existed and was still accepting sacrifices, she doubted he would come and pick up all that trash every evening after the idiots were gone.

"Miss Landon." Her personal guide joined her on the crowded platform. It was fenced off so people couldn't venture inside. "Do you not believe in sacrifice?"

"Ridiculous practice," she snorted. "I would rather sacrifice my life for Christ. I'm going to be a minister one day," she explained with pride. "Is there somewhere cool and quiet we can rest? I'm sick to death of this sweaty horde."

"Of course," Reed told her as he led her away. "There's a quiet pool a short walk down the river." His unusual golden eyes disarmed Selene. "You

191

won't tell anyone, will you? It's generally closed to the public."

Selene's heart fluttered. Mr. Piper was old enough to be her father, but so handsome! There was a definite animal attraction about him. Blonde fuzz covered his forearms where his sleeves were rolled up. It matched the gilded tuft that peeked from the top of his partially unbuttoned shirt. She melted every time he looked at her. Not that too many men looked at her. She didn't normally appreciate the attention of men. Her lips turned up slightly at the corners as her fingers fumbled with the top two buttons of her own shirt. It was sweltering out here, but the trip fit her budget at these off-season prices.

The pavement ended and soon the ground became uneven and rocky. Selene wore sensible shoes, but she was grateful when Mr. Piper helped her along the more rugged bits of terrain. She noticed they had travelled somewhat away from the river. "Mr. Piper..." she started.

"Please, call me Reed." he smiled and squeezed her arm. "Surely, we know each other well enough by now."

Three full days spent in the pleasant company of this man did seem like enough time. She shrugged, then conceded. "Reed, where is this pond?" She wasn't concerned, just curious. "This is quite a rough trail." It might have helped if she had paid more attention to the guide books and maps that her parents had given her in anticipation of this "trip of a lifetime" she had planned for years.

"Oh, it's not far now," he assured her. "There's a special place I thought you should see." He looked back at her as he pulled her up a small hill. "A secret place. I never take anyone here, but you seem like the kind of person that might appreciate it." A gentle squeeze of her hand inside his strong fingers sent a thrill through her midsection. "Besides, there is always a small price to pay for something extra special, no?"

She beamed back at him and said, "How thoughtful of you!" She felt she was really getting her money's worth on this trip.

Soon, a short walk through a cool, dim forest brought them to one of the most beautiful glades she had ever seen. The bright meadow was host to a multitude of flowers with butterflies and all manner of insects pirouetting from one blossom to another. Birds, in the trees behind them, serenaded her with their happy notes. Reed gently led her to the center of a heart-shaped fairy ring of pure white mushrooms. He sat and pulled her down beside him as he removed his backpack.

"We will eat soon, but the stream is just over that rise. Some cool water will quench our thirst," Reed told her.

He stood, his shadow throwing an unexpected chill across Selene's overheated body. Goosebumps rose in a surprise rush accompanied by an unfamiliar sensation. Electric ripples of ecstasy rolled like waves through her pelvis when Reed turned to look down upon her, his face dark with passion. Then he vanished and she was left alone as if time had frozen her in that wonderful/awful moment.

She came to her senses and lay back to catch her breath. The sun warmed her hair. Birdsong tinkled like flutes. She drifted, sleepy. The gold cross around her neck burned against her skin. Unclipped, it slipped from her fingers onto the ground unnoticed. Seduced by the blanket of heat that lay heavy on her, the distant music (*it can't be birds*) and the intoxicating perfume on the breeze, her eyelids drooped, but soon a tickling sensation woke her. Bees bumped against her as they bumbled along in their pollen gathering duties. She moved to brush them away, but more came. She struggled to keep her eyes open.

"Mr. Piper..." she slurred when his shadow fell over her. "Reed. The bees."

He bent over her and grinned. "Yes. You are their first and only and I will be yours."

Then they began to sting as they swarmed to cover her in a thick layer like a glistening coat of honey. "Please, help." She lifted her hand and when he didn't take it, looked up.

A strange man stood beside her. He was grotesque. Huge, muscular legs covered in fur ended impossibly as hooves. Small horns protruded from a heavy brow. She did recognize, however, the odd golden eyes.

The bee stings continued to penetrate her pure and perfect body. Selene's eyes glazed over as she released a final breath, but not before she beheld Pan's enormous phallus rise like a banner of triumph.

194

Love Letters

S J Townend

She couldn't resist its pull, its magnificence. Such royal splendour. It had been that way since childhood.

It stood outside the village store, five foot two of red cylindrical sexiness, shouting for her attention, unable to caress her from afar. It was anchored to the concrete, she had to put in all the work but she was happy when near it, even though it would never follow her home.

Monday to Friday at 8.45 and 5.15, she'd visit her unrequited love on her journey to and from work. She took the same route each day, the long route, so she could brush past it. Often she'd linger a little longer on a Friday afternoon by joining the queue for the counter. She'd line up with *Crochet Zone* magazine and a packet of humbugs, clasping the letter she'd scribed to anyone who could read. She'd crank her neck and stare.

She'd wait, caught up in erotica, until the shopkeeper was free to serve. The longer he took with the customers before her, the longer she spent with her love. She'd let others queue-barge until she was the last in line, until the sign needed to show 'closed' on a busy evening, until she was asked to leave. She would peek outside at its erect presence, at the tall pillar silhouette popping, throbbing against the light from the low slung afternoon sun. She'd pay for her goods and leave slowly, knocking something from a shelf on her way, hoping she'd timed her visit so she'd get to witness it being unlocked. opened up, emptied of its contents. This was what she loved to see. It made her wet with glee.

She felt the curvature and swing of its door call out to her as the postman turned his key. The throbbing in her chest and elsewhere rose to a crescendo as she watched him shuffle the envelopes from the post box's guts out and into a hessian bag and wished she could sneak in, take the place of the letters, curl up inside her Love.

Once it had been emptied, if no-one was looking, she'd ditch the magazine and sweets and leave the counter queue early to drift home—to witness such a sight was almost too much for one day. Before she left she'd brush her palms against the ring of bumpy, heavily painted protrusions cresting its neck just below its slit of an opening before grinding the warmth of her thigh against its bottom half if no-one from the shop was watching.

She was in love with the letterbox. For years she watched and touched it, caressed and felt it, filled it with letters to anyone, everyone and no-one. But she knew it was never to be.

She was broken hearted, withering on the vine, so eventually she settled for a man who adored phone boxes. They spent their weekends cycling around the cityscape, seeing how many pieces of government infrastructure they could spot and recorded their finds in a leather-bound book. For a while, he just about ticked her box.

Several years passed and she grew tired of the fakery, the sham marriage. All was far from well and a row broke out between the two, not for the first time. This day things turned physical as he threw a plate at the wall. He hadn't liked the dinner she'd cooked. She stormed off into the night, without shoes, keen to put distance between them. She pounded the streets in her house dress and slippers until all that shone was the moon and her feet leading her to the corner shop with the post box once more—her childhood sweetheart—and she felt she'd run far enough.

"You'll always love me, won't you?" she whispered and stroked its side. It agreed, silently. It was ghostlike, she saw through its inanimate disguise. She wrapped her arms around it and thrust herself against its cold, painted body, finding herself uninhibited by the blanket of night. The corner shop was closed, had been for several hours, there were no people, no one complaining about her ditching magazines without paying after she'd read them in the queue. This could only mean one thing—it was now or never.

She wanted to kiss her lover. She needed more than a kiss. She pressed her ruby red lips up against its neck and licked it. It tasted of vanilla and spice and everything her husband didn't. She couldn't hold back. Forty-nine years of repression. Forty-nine years of longing and lust. She slipped her fingers in its slit and then slowly, her whole hand. Before her rational thoughts could intervene, her left arm had slid inside, down the letterbox's throat. Ripples of pleasure rose up her body from her toes to the crown of her head. A swirling, a merry-go-round of passion spun in her solar plexus. She tipped her head back and exclaimed joy to the world, mouth open with ecstasy.

And then the post box closed its own lips—hard and tight on her arm. It ratcheted her in something like a ticker-tape timer and seized her hard at the shoulder. Its rectangular jaw cut and sliced and started to draw her torso through, too. Red blood and paint slid down its wall and into its core. She let out a piercing scream, eyes wide and rolling back into her skull, but her shriek was caught only by the wind of the night as the letter box swallowed her legs and feet. It spat out the slippers which fell to the concrete and, shortly after, her dress followed. In under a minute the screaming stopped. No-one came to her rescue.

Her body and limbs were blended and chopped and mashed and pressed in its guts; her organs were peeled and folded into letters. The postman came at eight forty-five, scooped out the guts and the lady who loved the letterbox was delivered all over the world.

Payback's A Bitch

Leslie Gulvas

Pete didn't see who tripped him, but he recognised the laughter. He had heard it often enough in the schoolyard. "Hey Dweeb, can't you walk?"

"Have a nice trip?"

They called themselves 'The Squad,' Bruce, Nick, Jake and Dean; the football team's defensive line. Being uniformly tall and muscular, they exuded entitlement. They also tormented Pete at every opportunity.

He checked the rip in the knee of his jeans. *Great, now I only have one pair I can wear to school.* His books were scattered. Nick kicked a couple into the bushes as he sauntered past. "Study hard, Dweeb."

This sort of ordeal was turning into a daily thing for Pete. Other kids were joining in the torture, trying to impress the top dogs. He'd tried talking to the Principal but it only made things worse. He'd even tried standing up to them in the park one weekend. Jacob and Bruce held him down and the other two beat him until his muscles cramped. He'd ended up with bruises all over his body. They'd taken his pants and left him. He had to hide in the brush and walk home after dark. His Mom had been passed out drunk on the couch when he came in. At least she didn't witness his shame.

Pete sorted his books. He was missing one from the library, an old one about witchcraft. He needed

199

it for research on his report about *The Crucible*. He crawled under the bushes, still hearing kids laughing out on the lawn. The book was open at the page *Invisibility Spell*. He fervently wished he could be invisible. He read the spell before he crawled out of the bushes. It wasn't too complicated.

When he got home, he found his Mom slurring her words already. The gallon vodka bottle on the table was half empty. It was going to be one of those nights. He went to his room to try to study, but she turned up the MTV and drunkenly sang along at the top of her lungs. The neighbors would be complaining soon.

Pete flopped on his bed. The library book fell to the floor, opening once more at the invisibility spell. He held his hands over his ears to deaden his Mom's Smirnoff fueled opera. His eyes kept straying to the spell.

"Why not!" he thought. He started gathering the things he needed for the spell. His Mom tried to get him to dance with her as he passed through the living room, but he shook her off.

"Party pooper," she slurred at him. She flopped on the couch and changed the channel to a daytime drama.

The easiest item to find for the spell was the big glass mirror. It had been in the basement ever since he could remember. Once all his supplies were laid out, he started the incantation, feeling a bit foolish. He burned the various items in the required sequence. The final steps would be the worst. He winced as he cut his palm. The blood pooled in his hand. He used it to copy the symbols from the book to the mirror. He chanted the complex phrases, each time more clearly and with more confidence. Just as the book said, the blood symbols started to smoke. It was working! Still chanting, he stuffed bay leaves in his nose and laid his hand on the mirror between the symbols. The mirror started to flow up his arm. As it flowed, his arm disappeared. He didn't even feel it on his skin. The mirror covered him completely apart from the leaves in his nose. He pulled them out and took a breath, looked down and couldn't see anything. Pete ran up the stairs and stood between his Mom and the TV. She didn't react at all, just kept watching her stories. Pete giggled, and she looked up blearily. "Wha," she slurred.

He patted her on the cheek and said, "Take a nap, Mom, you're hallucinating."

She hiccupped and settled back on the couch, mumbling incoherently.

Pete felt free. He decided to walk to Nick's house to see if he could mess with him a little. People passed him on the street and looked right through him. A woman walking a dog came so close he could've grabbed the leash. The dog didn't even notice him.

This is too cool, he thought.

Nick's house was in the best part of town. He was in the yard helping his father clean up fallen branches. They had one of those oversized chipping machines grinding up the wood to make mulch. Pete watched for a while comparing the beautiful house and yard to the shack where he lived.

Nick was working in clothes Pete would have saved for going on a date. Maybe losing a couple fingers in the wood chipper would show Nick life wasn't fair.

The next time Nick was pushing branches into the machine. Pete stood behind him and gave him a shove. Nick toppled forward.

The grinder caught his hand and pulled him face forward into the machine. His scream was drowned by the roar of the chipper. A red spray covered the wood chips. Nick bits shot out on to the mulch.

Pete felt a giggle rising in his throat. Oops, maybe he shoved a little harder than he meant to. He sauntered around to look at what was left. The asshole surely was shredded. A bit of an ear was next to a finger. White bone chips shone among the red splatter. An eyeball was next to Pete's foot. He picked it up and looked into it. "Fuck you, Nick. Who's a dweeb now?" He walked away. Behind him, Nick's father began to scream.

Jake's house was only a block over. Pete decided to surprise him with a third eye. The swimming pool in Jake's backyard was kidney shaped with a fountain at one end. Jake was there with several girls from school. Jake was running along the water's edge, showing off making flipping dives. "Watch this, a full back flip," he shouted, starting his run.

An invisible foot and a shove caused his momentum to throw him into the shallow end of the pool. The crack of his neck breaking hushed the girls' chatter. The water around Jacob's still form began to turn red.

The girls started to scream. He watched the commotion for a while. The girls' bathing suits left little to the imagination. The girls weren't as pretty as usual, their faces all screwed up from screaming and crying. Pete carefully placed Nick's eye on the table facing Jake's lifeless body.

He whistled as he walked to the bus stop, ignoring the confused looks of the people he passed.

"Two down, two to go," he whispered. Dean lived a couple of miles away. Pete jumped on the bus behind an old woman with a tightly curled cap of blue hair. The bus wasn't full, so he found a seat.

A ride for free was exhilarating. He amused himself poking the hair of the man in the seat in front of him. The guy kept slapping his head and turning to look for his tormentor. Pete had to cover his mouth to keep from laughing. This was great.

Pete let himself into Dean's house through the unlocked front door. It wasn't as fancy as Nick and Jacob's homes, but it was still nicer than the hovel he where he lived. Dean's mom was in the kitchen making dinner, no microwave food for Dean. She was even making peach cobbler. The smell was fantastic.

Dean was up in his bedroom. He had a fifty-inch TV and the newest Xbox. He played some game, shooting zombies, lounged on a king sized bed. The comforter matched the curtains. A half full bottle of sports drink sat next to him. Condensation glittered on the container. Pete thought about what he could do for a moment then a quick check of the bathroom yielded a bottle of drain cleaner.

While Dean was intent on zombie slaughter, Pete silently poured half the drain cleaner into the drink bottle. He leaned against the wall and waited. Ten minutes later Dean absently reached over and took a big swig of his drink. His eyes widened and he gasped, grabbing his throat. He staggered toward the door, croaking, "Mom!"

Pete shoved him back. Dean struggled, his face turning red as his throat swelled. His mouth gaped as he tried to draw air into his lungs. His struggles became weaker. When they finally stopped, his lips were blue and his bulging eyes had tiny red spots. He'd pissed himself too. "See ya in Hell, Dweeb," Pete muttered. He carefully replaced the drain cleaner and left as silently as he had come in.

The bus to Bruce's house was full, so he stood next to the driver. Pete amused himself flipping the light switches and opening and closing the door. The expression on the driver's face was priceless. The man finally stopped the bus to figure out what was wrong with his systems. Pete hopped off. He had a couple of blocks to walk, but he didn't mind. This one was going to be his most satisfying act of revenge. Bruce was crueler than the others.

Beatings and taunts were bad enough, but Bruce had orchestrated the worst torment of Pete's life. Somehow he found out Pete had a secret crush on Amy Snyder. He'd convinced her to agree to meet Pete for a date. The thought of the happy anticipation he'd felt standing in front of the mall wearing his best jeans was quickly followed by crushing pain. Pete's teeth ground, remembering Bruce's van driving up with the side door open, Amy taunting, saying she would never go out with a creep like Pete. Amy and the squad spread the story of his disgrace around school. Everyone but Pete had a good laugh for weeks.

Amy was dating Bruce now. She seemed to enjoy it when the squad tormented him.

Bruce was coming out of his house with his car keys when Pete walked up. He knocked the keys out of Bruce's hand. He scrambled for the keys while Pete popped the door and slipped into the back of Bruce's van.

They drove to Amy's house. She bounced into the van and kissed Bruce. Then drove to Sonic and got burgers and tots, the smell making Pete's stomach growl. Bruce and Amy didn't notice, they were singing along with the radio. The van came to a stop behind the barn on an abandoned farm. The two lovers climbed into the back of the van and Pete slipped out the back door.

"Damn," Bruce said. "That door must have been ajar the whole way here." He pulled the door shut.

Pete took a walk around the barn. He found a length of rope and a half full can of kerosene. A little later, the bouncing of the van and the giggling kept the occupants from noticing when Pete opened the driver's door to take the keys and Bruce's lighter. The rope went around the van through and around the door handles. It became quiet as he sloshed kerosene first over the front windows then the rest of the van.

"Bruce, what's going on? What's that smell?" Amy whispered.

Pete took off the gas cap and walked to the front of the vehicle where he lit the kerosene. He could see the lovers huddled under their clothes as the flames grew around the windows. Amy looked as good naked as he dreamed she would. Bruce was trying frantically to open the doors, but the hemp rope held. The windows were already alight with flames. Amy was shrieking continuously with teakettle intensity. The crashing inside slowed as the black smoke filled the van. Pete started walking toward the road as the screams ceased. He was a good quarter mile down the road when the gas tank exploded. No one could see his invisible smile.

He was hungry after the walk back to town. His Mom was passed out on the couch. An empty vodka bottle on the table told the story. The late news lit the TV screen. He saw pictures of Nick, Jacob and Dean. The commentator was talking about the tragic accidental deaths of three members of Washington High School's Bobcat football team. "Tragic my ass, deserved is more like it," Pete muttered. "They probably haven't found Bruce and Amy yet." He snickered. "Burnt and naked."

He went to the basement for the book of spells. He flipped through, looking for the one to make him visible again. There wasn't one. He looked through it again, nothing. He reread the spell he used. There was nothing about reversing the spell. "*Oh well,*" he thought. "*It will probably wear off. Most of the spells in the book end at dawn.*"

He went upstairs and made himself a ham sandwich. He was starving. He took the first bite and felt resistance as the sandwich entered his mouth. He bit down and felt something like gum around the food. The ham was unusually chewy, but he swallowed it anyway. Each bite was as chewy as the last. Mom always bought the cheap stuff. He took a drink of Coke. It went down his throat in a smooth glob, like a snot bubble.

His stomach was burning by the time he'd finished eating. He lay down on the tattered cover of his bed, but the pain was growing worse. He went to the bathroom and lay on the floor. The pain in his gut came in screaming waves. He vomited into the toilet. The bloody bile came out in a smooth bubble of glass, which shattered spewing blood when it hit the bowl.

***

The news van was set up on the school lawn.

"This is Bill Phillips reporting from Washington High School. Councilors are busy today, helping students cope with the loss of their friends. Six young lives lost in the course of just one day. All the deaths were under tragic circumstances. Nicholas Meyers killed in a wood chipper, Jacob Woszinski drowned in his swimming pool, Dean Sawyer unintentionally poisoned, Bruce Radner and Amy Taylor lost in a fiery auto accident. And finally, Peter Lowman bled to death after accidently ingesting broken glass. More on how the student body is coping with this tragedy on our eleven o'clock special report."

Tiny Fridge

Sheree Shatsky

Max is a hard man to slice. Damn muscle-bound steroid freak. Paula yanks the cleaver free from his ripped torso. Dull as a butter knife. She could use a good bone saw about now.

She throws open the kitchen drawer in search of anything sharper, digging past the plasticware and Burger King condiments, the twisty ties and knotted rubber bands. She settles on the carving set Max bought at the Williams-Sonoma outlet after Christmas, seventy-five percent off. He liked the Santa Claus head handles. *"Gen-u-ine North Pole,"* he said. Paula gives him a good kick and sticks what's left of him with the fork. "Ho ho ho, asshole."

She never should have killed him in the motor home. The fridge was way too small to keep him on ice. She'd told Max that morning making breakfast the fridge was tiny enough for Barbie's Dreamhouse. "Well, you sure as hell ain't no Barbie," he said, slamming back a protein smoothie with a splash of Jack. He smacked his lips with a *so good* smirk and she smacked him into hell fire eternity with the ease of cast iron.

Paula studies the frying pan covering his face, the underside greasy from eggs and bacon. She'd popped out his dead eyes because she couldn't stand him staring at her, sticking both in the egg compartment, facing the inside, so 'Ole Blue Eyes

209

could see for himself she was right all along about
the size of the fridge.

210

Death Wish

Edward Ahern

"The drain pipe's backed up again, Mr. Dimas, you have to send someone right away."

"I had it cleaned out six months ago! What are you putting through it?"

"Nothing. Your plumbing is no good. I've stopped paying rent until it's fixed. It's unlivable here."

Kirill muttered "God damn it!" into the cell phone, but then choked back his anger and tried reason. "Look Hend—ah, Jacob, the drain was repaired less than ten years ago and you'd agree it's worked perfectly up to now?"

"Up to now is history and ten years is enough time for roots to grow back into it. Fix it."

Another sub-human tenant bleeding off any hope of profit. "Look, Hendricks, there's nothing wrong with my plumbing. Whatever you're stuffing the drain pipe with, you have to clean it out yourself."

"I'm done fixing things that you should have, Dimas. Either you take care of it or I'll use the rent money to get it done."

"And I'll have you evicted."

"Good luck with that. It'll take you a year of paperwork and legal fees."

Kirill swore again. "Either fix it and pay the rent or you'll find out what I can do." He resisted the urge to throw his phone against his office wall and hung up. The familiar rage surged up from his belly.

"Curse you," he yelled. "Die after you're maimed in an accident." He tensed. His tenants were shiftless, but he'd never before hated one enough to curse him aloud. His expression hardened. He meant it. That money draining leech should cease to exist.

Both Kirill's hands were clenched into fists. He opened and flexed them, shifted his considerable mass in the chair and resumed processing receipts. Toward the middle of the afternoon, Lucy texted.

Need to see you this eve.

He texted back. *Absolutely. Looking forward to seeing more of you.*

The double entendre was deliberate. Kirill was slathering Lucy with innuendo to try and strengthen their affair. The technique was problematic. His few consummated relationships since his bitter divorce had been brief and ended badly, because, he told himself, he was attracted to complex women with issues. He knew that evening would be different.

He arrived at the bar fifteen minutes early and, as he waited forty-five minutes, Kirill's composure chipped into a jagged edge.

"There you are. Finally." He pushed out a smile.

Lucy was dressed in well-worn jeans and hoodie rather than date clothes. She sat, not next to, but across the table from him. After drinks had arrived, Kirill allowed Lucy two sips and a question about how her day had been before launching.

"Lucy, you know I'm seriously interested in you. I'd like to…"

She held her palm toward him. "No. Please stop, Kirill. I came tonight because you deserve to hear from me in person. I guess you're a good person, but—I don't know how else to say it—you unsettle me."

"Look, Lucy…"

"No, please let me finish. You're smart, well off and decent looking, but I'm not comfortable around you. I'm sorry, it's probably me, but we need to move on."

The anger crawled on crab legs up Kirill's throat. He blurted, "You bitch. Slurping down my booze, teasing me. Who the hell are you?"

Lucy started to say something, pressed her lips back together, got up and walked away. Kirill sat motionless and flushed for several seconds, then quickly downed his scotch and soda. He switched glasses with Lucy's and swigged her drink, the grapefruit juice rasping his throat.

He pulled out his cell phone, turned it on and started thinking up comments to trash her on social media. But he noticed a voice message. It was from Hendricks.

"Plumber comes in the a.m. If I spend my money you get reported to the Renters' Complaint Center."

"You runny dog turd!" The foursome at the next table turned their heads to stare at him. Kirill didn't care.

"I curse you, Hendricks. I curse you! I CURSE YOU!"

His waiter ran over to Kirill's table. "Sir, you must lower your voice or I'll have to ask you to leave."

"You can go to hell too. Forget a tip."

Kirill peeled a few bills from his money clip and tossed them on the table. Back in his car he forced himself to drive close to the speed limit. He knew if he let out the rage he'd be busted for speeding.

Once home, he microwaved and ate something mislabeled as edible. Then he loaded up a tumbler with scotch and ice and sat in front of a black TV screen nursing his drink and a black mood. Halfway through it he realized that his eyes were watering. *Dammit, Lucy, We could have been good for each other.* He finished his drink, washed the dishes and went to bed.

Kirill frequently dreamed, but could never remember much. Not that night. That night whatever dream he'd been wallowing in faded away to reveal a naked woman facing him. She had the body and face of a slender young woman, but gray hair that hung down straight from her head and pubis. The muscles on the woman's arms and legs were sharply defined. There was no visible fat on her and her face was as sharp boned as a model's.

"What the hell," Kirill dream-said.

"You may call me Nemma. Sister Nemma. You summoned me."

"I never..." Kirill hesitated. He hadn't had a wet dream in decades, but just maybe this was shaping up into one. "Sure. What did you have in mind?"

"You summoned me to execute a curse. I am prepared to do so. But be forewarned, this killing will be premeasured. If it is not warranted, the death will be on you."

The dream woman's expression was stony and Kirill figured his subconscious wouldn't let him nocturnally emit. "What? Who? Oh, you must mean Hendricks."

"Jacob Hendricks. Yes. Think carefully. You are about to sanction a murder. Be careful. Righteous anger is akin to measured love, the words do not fit together. Do you validate your curse?"

He hesitated again, caution surfacing, but knew the cheap scumbag would keep his rent money and report him for violations. Rage choked his dream voice.

"The bastard deserves to die. As soon as possible." Kirill felt himself smile.

The woman's face saddened. "Know that I take no pleasure in the deadly judgment between the two of you." And then, with no sound or vapor, she was gone.

Unlike his other dreams, the woman's words and image were still vivid to Kirill when he woke up. "I wish it were that easy," he said aloud. On an impulse he called Hendricks.

"Dimas, I just woke up from a horrible dream, about you and some woman. She mentioned your name and threatened to kill me. It was the worst nightmare I've ever had. She touched me and the pain was so intense I had to answer her. I woke up screaming. If I dream about her again it will kill me."

Kirill realized he was shaking. "Look, Hendricks, just pay the rent and repair."

"Not a chance," Hendricks hung up.

Kirill dressed and went to work. He occupied himself with the rental accounting until the receptionist called.

"Mr. Dimas, there's a Sister Nemma here to see you."

Fear chittered up through his chest. "Tell her to go away. I'm not available."

"Yes, Sir. OH! She touched me. I'm to tell you that she's on her way up."

Kirill jumped out of his chair and was halfway to the door when it opened. Nemma faced him. She wore leather sandals and a plain gray, sleeveless shift that hid the contours of her body. Gray hair shimmered around the expressionless eyes of a bird of prey.

"I am come to test the stone caster."

"How? Who?" Kirill flinched and backed up toward his desk.

She didn't seem to move, but was next to him and touched his cheek with her fingers. The left side of his jaw screamed with toothaches as his memories were sucked out into her fingers.

" Έτσι, η αλήθεια, thus the truth," she murmured, keeping her fingers softly to his face. "You have been found – wanting. I am come to exact the death you demanded."

Kirill yelled through the pain in his mouth. "But the curse is on Hendricks!"

"My decisions are two-edged swords, cutting as warranted. You have been judged. How do you

216

wish to remember your death?" She was silent for a heartbeat. " Ah. Very well."

Nemma's face filled in and re-formed. Kirill was staring at a sad faced Lucy with straight gray hair. "To what never really was but could have been, Kirill," she said and kissed him lingeringly on the lips. He passed in the fullness of that sensation.

The Bad Ones Are Always The Best

Michelle Ann King

Marty's grandson takes the cup of tea he's offered — without saying thank you, mind — and stares at it dubiously, as if he doesn't know what it is. Marty wouldn't be surprised if he doesn't; kids all seem to be brought up on vitamin water and kale juice, these days.

'Drink up,' he says, nodding encouragingly. Marty's cuppas are the real thing: brewed until they're the colour of brick dust and made with full-fat milk, four sugars and a thimble of whisky. 'It'll put hairs on your chest.'

Gary — no, *Garrett*; Marty's been corrected on that point at least twice already — doesn't seem impressed by the thought. No doubt he'd just have to wax them off afterwards, because God forbid he should spoil any of the smooth surfaces and rounded corners. The kid looks like he's been popped out of some kind of designer mould, all rough edges pre-sanded off. Model no. 87: Corporate Tax Consultant.

Marty can just imagine Robert and his snooty wife picking that one out of a catalogue. No wonder they kept their distance all these years; didn't want their perfect creation spoiled by messing about with an old man who used to work with his hands and misses the days when kids wanted to be astronauts and explorers when they grew up, not accountants.

Garrett puts his cup down — without using a coaster, the fucking heathen — and gives Marty a big Hollywood smile. In the living room's fading light, his whitened teeth go off like a flashbulb.

Marty returns the grin, giving it full dentures. The boy followed his nose here in the end, though. That's something.

Garrett turns his attention back to Marty's computer. He's offered to do his old granddad a favour and see if it needs updating, or cleaning up, or whatever. Starting with Marty's online banking account, he notices, before the kid angles the screen away.

'So,' Garrett says casually. 'Have you always lived around here, Granddad? In Silvertown? That's what it's called, where you were born?'

Marty nods and gives him an approving grin — although he can't help rolling his eyes a little, too. He might prefer life in the flesh — red in tooth and claw, and all that — to the dubious pleasures of the virtual world, but he still understands the concept of security questions. So while the lad gets points for initiative, he loses more for clumsiness.

Marty grins again. If Robert could see this, he'd be positively mortified. Not only has the kid reverted to undesirable type, but he's shit at it. 'That's right. Silvertown. All one word,' he adds helpfully.

The boy flashes another smile as he taps away, fingers flying over the keyboard. His nails are very short, very clean. Buffed. At his age, Marty would've been embarrassed to have manicured fingernails. His were always filthy and ragged,

219

broken in a dozen places from climbing and scrabbling and fighting.

It's different now, of course — these days, parents freak out if their precious kids so much as pop their heads outside the door without an armed security detail — but the past, as they say, was a different world.

Marty smiles. Literally.

'And did you have a pet, Granddad? What was it, the first pet you had?'

'Dog. Fierce little thing, he was. Half Pit Bull, half fuck knows what. Wolverine, maybe. Or hell hound.'

Another bright smile, another click of the mouse. 'Uh huh. And what was his name?'

Marty can't resist. 'Supercalifragilisticexpialidocious,' he says, then laughs as the boy's fingers go still and his eyes wide. 'I'm kidding. It was Killer.'

'Oh.' Garrett gives Marty an uncertain glance, then laughs too. 'Right.' His hands go back to the keyboard.

Marty dunks a Hob Nob in his tea. 'Don't suppose your dad ever got you a dog, did he?'

The kid shakes his head. 'I'm allergic.'

Of course he is. Tax consultants are bound to be allergic to anything beyond screens and numbers and climate-controlled offices. God forbid they should ever know the dirt and danger, the fun and freedom, of the real world. Or any other.

'You don't know what you're missing. We had some right good adventures in our day — like the time we found the portal.'

220

'Uh huh,' Garrett says, focused on the screen.

Marty smiles again. He'd been with Kenny and Eddie from down the street, playing cops and robbers on the local building site. They'd had the time of their lives, chasing Eddie's little brother over piles of bricks and rubble, through pipes, up scaffolding and down holes. *We'll get you, copper!*

'So we've got Joey cornered in this great big trench, where they're digging the foundations. It's over; there's nowhere for him to go. But when we jump in there, he's gone. There's all these roots, worms, bugs — big, weird bugs — but no Joey. We can't work it out. So Eddie's kicking at it, looking to see if there's some kind of tunnel or something and the next thing we know, he's gone straight through the wall and disappeared.'

'Uh huh,' Garrett says.

It'd come as a bit of a shock, of course, finding the portal. But once they calmed down, it made sense. For posh kids, yeah, doorways to other worlds would be found at the back of wardrobes stuffed with fur coats — but for the likes of Marty and his mates, they'd appear in dirty great holes in the middle of building sites. It made perfect sense.

'It was just like in the stories,' he says. 'Time was different on the other side. It felt like we were over there forever before we caught up with Ed. Before we found his little brother.' Or what was left of him, by that point. Again, this portal hadn't been like the ones in the kids' books.

It'd been much more fun.

'Where it went wrong,' he goes on, 'is that Kenny told people what really happened. Where we went, what we saw. What we did. Poor Ed never said a word — never spoke again, as far as I know — but Kenny told the truth.'

Which rarely does anyone any favours, honestly. Marty, who understood that, told the story people wanted to hear — or no, not really; nobody wanted to hear that kind of thing. But at least they could understand it.

Things weren't like they are now, with people seeing murderers and kidnappers on every street corner, but the concept wasn't exactly unknown, either. So Marty told everyone — his parents, the police, the doctors — about an old fella in a raincoat who asked them to help find his lost dog. He told them how Joey stayed searching after the rest of them got bored and went back to their game — until finally, they realised how long he'd been gone and went searching for him too.

It was a horrible story, yes — but the bad ones are always the best. And while people might not have been happy about believing Marty's version of events, at least they could. Which was a lot more than you could say about Kenny's.

'Uh huh,' Garrett says. He's frowning at the screen again, a disappointed expression on his face. Looks like he finally got into the accounts, then.

Marty takes pity. 'I wouldn't worry yourself about all that banking stuff,' he says. 'It doesn't matter if that's out of date, or whatever, because I don't really use it. Not a big fan of banks. Numbers on screens, and all that. I like proper money. Real money, that you can hold in your hand.'

The boy's head comes up. 'You mean... you keep your money in cash?' His gaze flicks around the room. 'In the house?'

'You haven't touched your tea,' Marty says reproachfully and Garrett obediently picks up his mug. He takes a mouthful, coughs violently, and just about manages a smile. 'Lovely, Granddad. So, er... you were saying?'

Marty nods. 'I was saying about my old mate Kenny, yes. In and out of nuthouses, hospitals and prisons for years, he was. Last time he got out, he came round here. He thought he was an exorcist or something, on a mission to rid the world of evil.'

Marty shakes his head sadly. Poor bastard. 'Nothing but skin and bone, he was. Said he was living on the nourishment of righteousness, or some bollocks. I gave him a nice cup of tea and a packet of custard creams. Perked him right up.'

Garrett shifts in his chair, all fidgety impatience. Kids have got no attention span, these days. No sense of commitment. In the old days, you picked a path and you stuck to it. Like Kenny, bless him. Like Marty himself.

'Of course,' he says, before Garrett can interrupt, 'then he tried to kill me and set the house on fire, so maybe inviting him for tea and biscuits wasn't such a great idea.'

The boy's eyes widen and he starts paying attention again. There's nothing like a bit of death and destruction to focus the mind.

'He realised, you see, about the house. I don't know how he worked it out, but he did. So of

223

course, he thought it was evil. Cursed ground, or something.'

Garrett looks confused. 'The house?'

Marty nods, gesturing around the room. 'This is where it was, you see. The portal. This estate, it's what they were building when we found it. That great big trench we were playing in, it was the foundations for this house. I watched it go up, brick by brick and wall by wall. Never forgot it. Worked like a mad bastard, I did, to get the money to buy it. Took fifteen years and some really dodgy jobs, but I got there in the end. Lived here ever since.'

'The... portal?' Garrett says. He still looks confused. That's what you get for not listening properly. Forgotten art, listening.

Marty listened to Kenny, when he came round. He ranted and raved for days about what it'd been like over there — about evil, and monsters and all manner of horrors. And Marty listened to every word, because they'd been mates and because he felt sorry for the poor bastard — nobody else had ever believed him.

Plus, he found the whole thing pleasantly nostalgic. His own memories had already started wearing a bit thin from repeated fondling by then, so it was quite nice to get a fresh perspective.

'What happened to him?' Garrett wants to know. 'Kenny?'

'Nobody knows,' Marty lies. 'He'd done a runner by the time the police turned up. They never found him.'

That part, at least, is true. Again, it was different in those days: they didn't have all that high-tech CSI stuff, fibres and databases and DNA. And Marty was a fine upstanding homeowner while Kenny Rudow was a known offender with no fixed address and a history of mental illness. Case closed.

For a while, Marty had hoped Kenny might turn out to be the missing ingredient, the key that would turn the lock, but no joy. He'd been trying his damnedest ever since he'd moved in, obviously — begging, pleading, bringing it offerings — but even when he brought it Kenny, he got nowhere. The portal stayed shut.

Later he started wondering if it was an age thing: if it only opened for kids. Which was a trickier theory to test, since a single man living on his own didn't get much cause to invite children to come and play in the hole underneath his floorboards. And unlike homeless nutters, kids would get missed.

It'd be easier if he had his own, he realised in the end — hence Janice, and then little Robert.

But Robert wasn't exactly an adventurous kid, that was the trouble. Not exactly a chip off the old block. He never wanted to play cops and robbers, or soldiers, or even underground explorers. He cried at the slightest bruise, was terrified of bugs and knives and anything with teeth and practically fainted at the sight of blood. If the boy hadn't been the spit of him physically, Marty would've done some serious questioning of Janice's virtue.

He finishes his tea with a slurp and fishes out the soggy remnants of biscuit with his finger. He did think about having another go, but Janice had started to cause trouble by then and the whole thing had been such hard work and such a disappointment, that he couldn't face going back to square one. So he let Robert grow up and go his own way — he became a poet, just to add one final humiliation — and mostly gave up on trying to get the portal open. Mostly.

But now there's Garrett and it feels as if maybe he's being given one final chance. The boy's older than he would have liked and an idiot, but he's still got Marty's blood in his veins. And he's at least got a bit more oomph than his father. Cyber fraud, or whatever you'd call it, isn't exactly Most Wanted stuff, but it isn't poetry, either. Maybe there's hope for the kid, with the right encouragement. The right environment.

Maybe the portal will think so, too.

Garrett does an elaborate stretch and stands up. 'You get stiff sitting down too long, don't you, Granddad? Maybe we could walk about a bit — you could give me a tour of the house, if you like.'

'Good idea.' Marty snaps his fingers, as if he's just had the thought. 'Here, why I don't I show you where I keep the money? You can tell me if you think it's safe enough.'

'Okay, sure. I'm happy to help.' Garrett gives him another smile, although it's less dazzling this time. The pills dissolved in his tea are probably starting to make themselves felt.

'It's right this way,' Marty says. 'In the back room, under the floorboards. You might have to get down there and dig around for a bit, though. You haven't got to rush off, have you? Your dad not expecting you home?'

Garrett yawns and shakes his head. The smile turns a little conspiratorial. 'I didn't actually tell him I was coming to see you.'

Marty grins and slaps the kid soundly on the back, hard enough to bruise. Garrett winces and lets out a surprised *oof*, but at least he doesn't start crying. Good lad.

'Chip off the old block,' Marty says happily, with a little touch of pride — and hope — in his heart.

Where Only the Mosquitoes Sing

Dan Allen

Old folks say it is only a myth to entertain the youth, but if you visit a certain northern lake in the calm of the night when the moon is new and the loons are silent and a whisper can be heard for miles, you might experience something that will change your mind faster than a bullfrog's tongue snapping up a mayfly.

In a land where you can peel the skin off the white birch and each year moose shed their antlers and black flies grow big enough to carry away a squirrel, there is a tale of a star-crossed romance, tender young hearts brought together by attraction and divided by tragedy. At Camp Chikopi, nestled between pine trees on the eastern shore of Ahmic Lake, the boys retell the story, passing it from generation to generation. The legend grows with each batch of new campers, whispered inside musty cabins after the lights are out. Across the gentle waves and just beyond where the cold waters flow from the mouth of the Magnetawan, young girls at Camp Wathahi share a similar tale, spreading the heebie-jeebies and keeping themselves up late at night.

The story begins with hyper teens paddling across the lake, gliding over sun-sparkled waters, to visit each other's grounds. They compete like rabid chipmunks, they burn off endless energy in a revolving series of games until darkness fills the

228

eastern horizon and a nightly campfire ends the day. Then, snuggled close to warm flames, enticed by the sweet aroma of burning hardwood and blanketed by the haze of smoke spiralling heavenward, a boy makes eye contact with a girl and smiles.

Caught in the trance of hand-holding puppy love, the two scheme to rendezvous at midnight in the cove beneath the cliffs on the thick evergreen-covered north shore, planning to seal their attraction with a first kiss.

When the cabin councillor's snore shakes dust from the rafters and his fellow campers are dreaming of ice cream and cellular reception, the boy creeps away and slips a canoe into the lake. Careful not to splash, he manipulates the paddle with the expertise of a fur-trading voyageur traversing the meandering waters of Algonquin.

He stops halfway and sits abreast of Harlow's Cove. His canoe bobs on gentle waves,and he watches as the dark outline of his first love approaches. Her smooth strokes slice through the midnight mist and her hair catches a faint reflection of the eyelash-shaped moon.

The boy stands to wave at his newfound love and guide her into the covert shadows beneath a protective cliff that provides them with the privacy of a limestone curtain. His sudden movement causes a tilt and water threatens to pour over the side. He shifts his weight in a frenzied reaction and the unbalanced canoe capsizes quicker than the flash of a shooting star. Tossed into cold ink water, the boy loses his way and drifts to the bottom.

With tears in her eyes and a flashlight, gripped in shaking hands, the young lady finds only a paddle and the upside-down fibreglass hull. The search ends after fruitless days of dredging the bottom and poking around the submerged fallen trees and driftwood-littered shoreline. The boy is never found, his remains never buried, but each year with the melting of the ice and the return of the robins, boats are untethered and set adrift on moonless nights and paddles disappear from cabin porches as he makes his presence known.

Recently, three young lads with curly blond hair and apple pie smiles escape from their paved-over world of cement and glass and pick the cliff in Harlow's Cove to camp for the night. When their fire burns low and the northern lights shimmer like a dancing green glow-worm, after the cookies are consumed and hockey opinions debated, one restless camper dares the rest to jump off the cliff. In the kingdom of boys and double-dog dares, he has no choice but to take the first leap. The darkness hides his descent, but the splash alerts his pals and anything that might be stirring below the surface. The boy torpedoes deep and struggles to reverse his plunge. Cold hands grasp a leg, and bones pinch his skin, dragging him deeper. The terrified boy kicks with an urgency only fear can evoke and the hands holding him slip towards his ankles, scratching him with the fleshless tips of decomposing fingers.

Free at last, his legs burn from spent adrenaline and his lungs, drained of air, threaten to implode like a crushed pop can. He pulls at the water above and thrashes with the frenzy of a cat tossed into a

230

bathtub. Nearing unconsciousness, he breaks through the surface into sweet midnight air and swims towards shore with one last desperate flurry. Certain his attacker is mere inches behind, his heart pounds faster with each panicked stroke. He senses the creature getting closer and closer and holds his breath, saving his air for a final death scream. Finally, his knee touches a moss-covered stone and he drags himself out into a chilling breeze and scrambles, shivering, climbing to the safety of the cliff above.

His pals smirk and steal glimpses at each other as he tells his tale, not believing the drama of his experience nor his near-fatal escape. Between whispered doubts and muffled chirps, they lay him on a sleeping bag and their battery-powered torches chase away phantoms and expose shadows. Like a spotlight on a stage, a circle traces the scratches from above his knee to his ankle. Five distinct ragged marks scar his pale leg and the cuts begin to darken as if they wear lipstick. At the bottom of the longest line, something grey and ugly sticks out of the gash. The pals move in close, their noses almost touching, to see a sight that promises to haunt their sleep. They flinch and the flashlight slips between frozen fingers, blinking out against the ground. They hurry to turn back on the light, not believing the horrifying implications of what is protruding from the wound. Their fears are confirmed. Hooked under the skin, all algae-covered, gnarled and twisted, is an old fingernail.

In the warmth of the early summer, when the mosquitoes hatch and the horseflies swarm, busloads of youth leave behind the monotony of their urban lives and return to a northern paradise, stirring the lake with the roar of laughter. In the dark blue of a shadowed bay, a canoeist's stroke slaps the surface and wakes a dormant spirit for another year of haunting the waters, searching for a lost love and a missing paddle. If you're ever fortunate to stand on a soft blanket of pine needles and marvel at the sight of more stars than you ever could imagine and if you hear, in the dark moments near midnight, a loud splash that carries over the lake, then put away the paddles, drag up your boat and stay out of the water, for you won't be alone if you dare take a swim on a moonless night, in a northern lake where only the mosquitoes sing.

The Day Death Wore Boots

Dorothy Davies

The thing is ... I'm old enough to know better, old enough to know it isn't a good idea to stand looking in the window of an 'antique' shop and be taken in by a toy.

It's not like I'm lonely, is it? I mean... I got a life, ain't I? Course I have. Go to work, talk to people, shop, talk to people, come home, cook my TV dinner which I eat in front of the computer – all right, I'm lonely.

But that's beside the point, really it is. I wanted the toy cos I wanted the toy, not because I don't have a life.

I've always loved Westerns, you see, the whole shoot-'em-up gunfights and ranches and outlaws and everything. And there's this toy, a whole town of it, a Western town with gunfighters and horses and ladies wearing flouncy dresses who are no better than they should be and there's the cattle outside the town and the cowboys bringing them in and there's the sheriff and the undertaker standing by because of the gunfight in the street and the men leaning on the bar outside the saloon and the whole thing was taking up the entire window display and I wanted it.

It would be silly money, of course, but I had silly money, not having much else to spend it on these days. No wife, no lover, no – nearly said it, didn't I? Nearly said 'no friends.' Well, it would be true.

So I went in and saw the old man selling the thing and said I wanted it. And he said no. It wasn't for sale. And I said, "oh yes it is; it's right there in the window and no sign to say DISPLAY ONLY and I want it."

And he says; this old guy with a peaked cap and twisted smile and when he turned, a big hump on his back like you would not believe, a true hunchback, poor guy and I wondered if it pained him at times, a twisted spine like that, he says:

"It's dangerous. I sell it and it comes back later with an addition. One I don't always like."

"Addition? Explain yourself, sir."

"Well, the sheriff wasn't there when I got it first off; he was there when it came back in. The gunfight wasn't there, now I'm worried that there's going to be a death, or something."

I laughed. I laughed until my stomach hurt.

"It's like model trains," I gasped eventually, when the convulsions stopped. "You add things as you go along."

"Maybe," he said, obviously unconvinced. "Maybe, but there's this – light that comes over the thing and it changes."

"I still want it," I said, determined to have it at all costs. A childhood dream, my own Western town to play with! Adult I might be, child I was inside. As we all are.

He shrugged. "I have to put up the arguments," he said. "If the customer persists, then I let them buy it. It's £2,500."

234

"Done."

He looked at me in shock. "You're not going to haggle?"

"No. I said I wanted it and I meant it."

"All right. Don't know how much I'll be able to give you when you return it, though."

"Return it? It's mine to keep forever!"

"I don't think so. No one's kept it yet and they all said that."

"I'm different."

"They said that, too."

The mood in the shop changed subtly; a darkness crept in, a hint of – menace. I shivered and pulled out my platinum credit card. Best get this purchase done and dusted, I thought, and be out of there, taking my dreams of future evenings of happiness away with me.

The old man took the card as if it would explode in a moment of madness. "You sure about this?"

"I'm sure."

"Be it on your head, then."

The card transaction was soon done. How quickly and easily we can spend money with plastic! In olden days I would have counted out the money and he would have counted it again or I would have produced a gold nibbed fountain pen and written a cheque in an elegant italic hand. Instead I punched four numbers into a machine and it churned out a soulless slip of paper in return.

I wrote my address on the pad he offered me and arranged a delivery time for the following

Saturday. I left the shop with his strange words in my ears and my mind.

"You'll be all right if you don't see the ghost light, Mister."

I almost turned back, almost wanted to grab him by the lapels and say 'if you don't want to sell the bloody thing, don't display it! Don't try and frighten people with silly notions! Take the money and be glad of the sale! Don't you know there's a recession in place?'

I didn't. I walked away, quickly. I walked away because I thought if I asked questions about the ghost light there might be answers I didn't want to hear. Or I would do some damage and the sale would be cancelled.

I wanted the Western town to play with.

I admit it. I had not grown up. Not by a long, long way.

***

Saturday was a long time coming.

It was Wednesday when the purchase was made. I had all of Wednesday evening, all of Thursday's endless 24 hours and all of Friday's 24 hours to live through and then, heaven help me, most of Saturday to get through, too. Impatient to have my Western town? Of course not. In denial, I know that.

But eventually the removal van was there. Four big overweight red faced men got out and began manhandling my precious town off the pallet it was on and working out how to get it over and around my garden gate, my front door, my stairs... but they did it with great ease and I wondered how many people had owned this precious toy before me and how many times it had been returned... I didn't want to ask. I didn't need to know. It was mine and that was all there was to it.

I had cleared the second bedroom for the town, arranged tables so that it would be at the right height for me to observe it. Do please note I did not say 'play with it', not then. I said it earlier but not when it arrived. Then it was serious. A hobby. An interest. Not a game.

They placed it on the tables. They gave me a box which they said held the people, horses and cattle. They bid me a happy time with my new acquisition and they left, declining any invitation to drink tea or coffee or alcohol. It was as if they could not wait to be free of the thing.

I shut the front door behind them and raced back upstairs, eager to place the people and animals in my new town.

They were already there. The box was on its side, the cattle were outside the town, the horses were tied up in front of the saloon, the men were leaning on the rail - ready to watch the gunfight which was about to take place.

I decided I was seeing things. I decided none of it was real; I had all evening to put everyone where I wanted them.

It was clear that the toys/dolls/whatever they were had other ideas.

Even as I stood there, open mouthed, the two confronting each other in the middle of the main street pulled their guns and fired. One fell down in a puff of smoke and dust.

I left the room.

I left the room to go find a bottle of whiskey and have several stiff drinks.

I did not see what I just saw. I did not see the dolls/toys/whatever they were actually do something by themselves.

I decided that I had to make statements which I would believe.

So I believed that they had not put themselves into the town.

They had not walked, talked and done something in front of me without my help.

Had they?

I went back upstairs, curiosity getting the better of me. Surely they were playacting, surely one had not been –killed – had it?

It was as if I wasn't there. None of this 'freezing when a human walks into the room' as we are led to believe 'real' toys did.

It was as if ... this town was real life. As I walked in the room I saw someone bending over the man on the ground, shaking his head. The undertaker wandered over and pulled out a tape measure. I couldn't believe it. He really was dead. He had to be. He hadn't moved, even when pushed around a bit. The man who had killed him had walked off. He was nowhere to be seen.

They talked. I know they talked, I saw their mouths move. I couldn't hear a word but I knew everything they were saying.

"He's a gonner, ain't he, Doc?"

238

"That he is."

"Do we know who he is?"

"Nope. Best get him buried in Boot Hill and hope no one comes asking. Big Dan's done it again."

I left the room for the second time. I had to be going out of my mind. There was no other explanation.

It took a good deal of courage for me to walk into the room again. Curiosity drove me there and the need to see the toy on which I had spent over £2000 helped me overcome my fears – to some degree.

I opened the door and edged in carefully. The men were gone from the saloon, the horses had gone too. The cattle had disappeared. No one was lying in the road. All was calm. It looked like a toy once again.

Except for the strange misty white light surrounding the whole thing.

Except for the blood stain on the sand in the middle of the road.

Even as I thought about it, a man came out of the saloon, walked across to the spot and kicked sand over it. He walked back into the saloon, the door swinging open just enough for me to see all the men at the bar and the tables, some gambling, some laughing, all drinking. The floozy behind the bar waved to me. I swear she did.

I remembered what the hunchback said about the 'additions' to the town each time it came back. There would be 'additions,' he said.

239

The truth was, this town was real, tiny but real and people would come and go. Even realising that, I could not come to terms with the fact I had seen a real gunfight and a real death.

A cart came creaking along the road, a rough pinewood coffin on the back. Two men walked alongside, carrying spades. They were going to bury the dead man.

Money or not, I went nowhere near the town for the whole of Sunday. I sat in my lounge with whiskey and loud music but it didn't muffle the sound of horses, wheels, cattle, men shouting, the occasional gunshot, shrieking giggling women and the ominous sound of spades hitting earth. I told myself it was all in my head. I told myself it was my wild imagination, everything I had ever read, watched, thought of, was happening right there above my head. In my mind.

It was in my mind, wasn't it?

Monday morning curiosity got the better of me. I went slowly up the stairs, afraid of walking around my own home. That was ridiculous. It was outrageous. I had spent good money on a toy and I wanted to play with it.

Said it for the first time, didn't I? Play with it. The hunchback hadn't told me I would be an observer to real life happenings. He treated it as an expensive toy.

Perhaps he didn't know.

What was the 'ghost-light' he was on about? I had to find out.

The town was quiet. There was one horse outside the General Store. It stood still, well, sort of, it was busy dropping turds into the road actually and I wondered, even as I watched, why no turds were seen in Western films. Did they hire someone specifically to clear them up the moment a horse dropped them? What sort of job was that? What sort of money would they get?

Someone came out of the General Store carrying a weighty saddlebag, the way it pulled him down one side it had to be heavy. He mounted the horse and rode out of town. Gone. Over the edge of the board the town was on and gone. Into – what?

There was mystery on mystery here.

I did what I should have done in the first place, got me a comfortable chair and sat down to watch the show.

The Sheriff's office door opened and he sauntered out, cigarette in the corner of his mouth, Stetson at a jaunty angle. He stood on the sidewalk/boardwalk/whatever and surveyed the empty road. It was as if he was waiting for someone/something, rather than keeping a watchful eye on the inhabitants of –

The town had no name. I had just realised that, with a shock. I could call it Dodge City but that would be too silly for words. I needed my own name.

"Smoke Town," I said aloud.

The sheriff turned round on his bootheels and glared at me.

"In the name of God, Mister, what sorta dang-fool name is that?" he shouted.

"Sorry." I waved a pathetic hand in his direction. "What's the town called, then?"

"Ghostlight."

I felt a shudder run the length of my spine. You can't call a town Ghost Light, surely?

"It's Ghostlight, Mister, all one word." The sheriff looked at me as if disbelieving I could be that stupid. Well, I guess I was; I bought the thing, after all. "And..." he added, taking off the Stetson and scratching his head, "you ain't dressed proper, either. Where's your chaps and Stetson and six shooter, then?"

"I..."

I left the room. I left not because I was disconcerted by an idiotic conversation with a sheriff who was a doll, an extra in a toy Western town, but because I had an overwhelming desire to 'dress proper'. I headed for my town, where people were a normal size and spoke in normal voices and took money for goods and they took my money for a complete Western fancy dress outfit, including gun and boots. The gun, they assured me, was a replica, which they were not supposed to sell under new gun laws but which they slid into the package because no true-blue-up-and-coming cowboy would be seen out without one.

I agreed.

I hurried home through the blazing sunshine, through the shoppers indifferent to my excitement and my anticipation and my fears, rushed into my house and went to change.

242

Properly fitted out, looking every inch the rough roustabout cowboy, I went back into the room to look at Ghostlight. My western town. My purchase. My possession.

If I said it often enough I would believe it – eventually.

The sheriff was sitting in a beat up old chair, balancing on the back legs which looked like they'd give way any minute. He looked up when I walked in and grinned.

"Better. Now Big Dan can come into town and meet you proper. He wouldn't want to see no dandy, would he?"

I sat down in my chair. "How much of this place does Big Dan own?"

"Most on it." The sheriff sucked on a cigarillo for a bit and then turned back to me. "How come no one else asked these questions, Mister? I mean, we been in some homes, for sure we have, but no one asked questions."

"What did they do, then? Just watch?"

"Nah. Run screaming from the room more times than not. You ain't done that. You're different."

I laughed. I could well understand people running screaming from the room. I had not exactly run but left rather sharp-ish a few times. "I'm intrigued," I told him. "How do you live and do things without what I can see as physical conditions?"

"Like?"

"Well, water and food and..."

243

"You got it wrong, Mister. Truth is; this is a town in a state in a country. You got just one bit of it, like a window, if you like."

"So, the gunfight was real, then?"

"Course it was. Damn outlaw coming into town looking for trouble, got shot down and got buried."

"Shot down by..."

"Big Dan."

"Does he really own this town?"

"Sure enough does." The sheriff got up and stretched. "I'm through chattering, Mister. You got enough to think on for a while. I'm about to go get me a drink or two. I see old Ned heading this way on his ass; he's always good for a story or two. You ain't got no stories, Mister, just a load of questions. You'd be better done watching and not asking."

He ambled across the sandy road just as Old Ned, whoever he was, came into view on the far edge of the town – as far as I was concerned, anyway. Judging by the state of him, he'd travelled a good deal further than that.

I watched the old man shamble into the saloon; saw the sheriff greet him and as the doors swung back with a clatter – they were badly fitting doors, someone should sort that out for them – I saw the drinks being poured.

And I waited.

The singing started, then the fights, usual problems I expect in a Western town. Bodies spilled from the saloon into the street, spitting, fighting, falling down drunk but no one pulled a gun.

At that point, anyway.

That sort of came later.

You must forgive me; I am not entirely sure what happened then. I know I was tired and hungry and needed a bathroom visit and was reluctant to leave the town in case I missed anything.

Then I saw this guy, drunk as a skunk, for want of a better polite expression, staring at me.

"What you think you're looking at?" he snarled.

"Well, the town..." I answered, a bit sheepishly. Seemed a silly answer but it was the truth.

"Get yourself gone!" he snapped.

"I can't do that," I protested. "I bought this town and I'm entitled to look at it if I want!"

"Really?" He showed yellowing teeth in what passed for a grin. It didn't work. "The man with the gun says who's entitled!" and damned if a bullet didn't whistle past my ear and bury itself in the ceiling.

In a moment I pulled my gun and fired back.

And he fell down dead.

I stared at him. Stared at the 'replica' gun and wondered what the hell had just gone down there. And why.

The sheriff came out and looked at the dead man, then at me.

"Oh my," he said, so soft I hardly heard him."That's Big Dan's brother, Mister. You're in trouble now."

"It was ... they said ... supposed not to be a real gun ..."

It all sounded false even as I said it.

I knew he wouldn't believe me. Hell, *I* did didn't believe me, either.

I turned out the light and left the room before the misty ghostlight came and bothered me.

So you see, friend, if you've got all that down in your notebook, that's how it happened. Honest to God that's how it happened.

I got up next morning and found bars on my bedroom window and a lock on the door.

And the padre came to see me. Why was I not in the least surprised to see it was the hunchback from the toyshop?

He gave me a lopsided sort of smile. "It's coming back to me again, then," he said, looking round the room, swinging the bunch of keys from one finger. "With another addition."

"What's that?" I asked, stupidly, I should have known the answer.

"A gallows," he said. "They're hanging you in the morning."

Grateful thanks to Yul Brynner who donned his Westworld outfit and came to stalk my office floor and dictate this totally insane story with the evil grin he wore throughout that film. The rest of the time he's one very nice person...

Meet the authors

Ed Ahern resumed writing after forty odd years in foreign intelligence and international sales. He's had over three hundred stories and poems published so far, and six books. Ed works the other side of writing at Bewildering Stories, where he sits on the review board and manages a posse of six review editors.

https://www.twitter.com/bottomstripper
https://www.facebook.com/EdAhern73/?ref=bookmarks
https://www.instagram.com/edwardahern1860/

Dan Allen is Canadian and enjoys spending time in Northern Ontario. You can find his short stories in numerous magazines, anthologies, and podcasts. Visit www.danallenhorror.com to see a presentation of his published work.

His terrifying look at Alzheimer's, "Above the Ceiling," is featured in Bards and Sages collection of the Best Indie Speculative Fiction Vol. 2.

A personal favourite, "Sympathy for the Zingara," can be found in the March 2019 edition of ParAbnormal Magazine.

His terrifying story, "The Basement" (edited by Horror Zine's Jeani Rector), was published by Hellbound Books in July 2020.

You can visit Dan at www.danallenhorror.com and follow him on Facebook and Twitter at @danallenhorror. You can write to Dan at contact@danallenhorror.com

Olivia Arieti lives in Torre del Lago Puccini, Italy, with her family. She writes drama, poetry and fiction. Her stories have appeared in several magazines and anthologies including, *Enchanted Conversations, Enchanted Tales Literary Magazine, Fantasia Divinity Magazine, Forgotten Tomb Press, Horrified Press, Infective Ink, Pandemonium Press, Sirens Call Publications, Blood Song Books, Black Hare Press, Pussy Magic Magazine, Stormy Island Publishing, Breaking Rules Publishing, Scarlet Leaf Review, Iron Faerie Publishing, Dark Dossier Magazine, Paramour Ink Press, Raven and Drake Publishing.*

Diane Arrelle has more than 350 short stories published and two short story collections: Just A Drop In The Cup and Seasons On The Dark Side. She, and her sane husband and insane cat, live on the edge of the New Jersey (USA) Pine Barrens (home of the Jersey Devil).
www.arrellewrites.com FaceBook: Diane Arrelle

Gary Budgen lives and works in London. His previous work has appeared in various magazines including Interzone, BFS Horizons, Morpheus Tales, Sein und Werden and the BFS Award short-listed anthology Humanagerie from Eibonvale. His work has been in many other anthologies from publishers including Thirteen O'Clock Press, Boo Books and Horrified Press. A collection of stories, Chrysalis, is published by Horrified Press and the chapbook Fragments of Onyx by Salo Press. A full publishing history can be found at garybudgen.wordpress.com.

Alaric Cabiling is an author and producer living in Manila, Philippines. He resided in Richmond, Virginia, United States, for seventeen years and much of his work takes place there. Ukiyoto Publishing House recently published his collection of stories, Il Migliore Del Mondo & Other Stories on June 2, 2021. He is disabled and identifies as gay.

Dorothy Davies is an editor, writer, photographer and medium. Somehow all these things come together in her seemingly crowded leisure and work life. She is an avid kindle user and delights in writing reviews for Amazon, especially when a novel is deleted a mere 2-3 chapters in and is too badly written to be read… she retired from editing for a while to run a second hand shop, the best one on the Isle of Wight, but the thrill of finding and publishing outstanding stories became too much so she started again with the Gravestone Press imprint. She still runs the shop…

Elana Gomel is an academic with a long list of books and articles, specializing in science fiction, Victorian literature and serial killers. She is also a fiction writer who has published more than ninety short stories, several novellas and three novels: *A Tale of Three Cities* (2013), *The Hungry Ones* (2018) and *The Cryptids* (2019). Her story "Where the Streets Have No Name" was the winner of the

2020 Gravity Award, and her story "Mine Seven" is included in *The Best Horror of the Year 13*.
She is a member of the Horror Writers of America.
Her website is:
https://www.citiesoflightanddarkness.com/
She can also be found on social media:
Facebook https://www.facebook.com/elana.gomel
Twitter https://twitter.com/ElanaGomel
Instagram https://www.instagram.com/elanagomel/

Donna L Greenwood writes flash fiction, short stories and poetry. Her work has been nominated for Best Small Fictions and Best Microfiction. Her debut novelette-in-flash 'The Impossibility of Wings' has recently published by Retreat West.

Michelle Ann King is a short story writer from Essex, England. Her stories of fantasy, science fiction, crime, and horror have appeared in over a hundred different venues, including *Strange Horizons, Interzone, Black Static*, and *Orson Scott Card's Intergalactic Medicine Show*. Her collections are available in ebook and paperback from Amazon and other online retailers, and links to her published stories can be found at her website: www.transientcactus.co.uk

Robert Allen Lupton is retired and lives in New Mexico where he is a commercial hot air balloon pilot. Robert runs and writes every day, but not necessarily in that order. More than a hundred and seventy of his short stories have been published in several anthologies including the New York Times best seller, "Chicken Soup For the Soul – Running For Good". His novel, "Foxborn," was published in April 2017 and the sequel, "Dragonborn," in June 2018. His first collection, "Running Into Trouble," was published in October 2017. His next collection, "Through a Wine Glass Darkly," was released in June 2019. His newest collection, "Strong Spirits," was released on June 1, 2020.

His third novel, "Dejanna of the Double Star," was published in December 2020.

His edited anthology, "Feral: It Takes a Forest to Raise a Child," was published September 1, 2020.

Robert has been an active Edgar Rice Burroughs historian, researcher, and writer since the 1970s. His contributor page, including several of his articles, stories, and over 1100 drabbles, on the ERBzine website is: https://www.erbzine.com/lupton/.

Chris Marchant currently lives in the Normandy region of France with her partner and far too many cats. She writes mainly science fiction, fantasy and historical, but veers off course now and then. She is currently working on an historical Gamelit/LitRPG novel. Her website is www.chrismarchantwriter.com. She also has guardianship of #Drizztthemusecat.

Terrance V. Mc Arthur is a storyteller, puppeteer, magician, balloon artist, basketmaker, and a retired librarian. His stories have been anthologized by Thirteen O'clock Press, Untreed Reads, and Trembling With Fear.

Chris Rodriguez has retired from the horrors of conventional life. She now lives on the brink of inspiration in a 100-year-old cottage in Pocatello, Idaho. Her works have appeared in various themed anthologies including Rhetoric Askew, several by Horrified Press/Thirteen O'Clock, Left Hand Publisher's, *Mindscapes Unimagined*, ParABnormal Magazine, DL Russell's *Nobody Goes Out Anymore* and Blunder Woman Productions, *Wrong Turn,* which has recently won Best Audiobook Anthology at the SOVAS Awards. You can find her latest at https://www.chrisrodriguez-onthebrink.com____or https://www.amazon.com/author/chrisrodriguez-onthebrink.

Rie Sheridan Rose multitasks. A lot. Her short stories appear in numerous anthologies, including Killing It Softly Vol. 1 & 2, Hides the Dark Tower, Dark Divinations, and On Fire. She has authored twelve novels, six poetry chapbooks, and lyrics for dozens of songs. She is also editor-in-chief for Mocha Memoirs Press and editor for the Thirteen O' Clock imprint of Horrified Press. She tweets as @RieSheridanRose.

Sheree Shatsky writes wild words. Her work has appeared in a variety of journals in print and online. Read more at shereeshatsky.com

SJ Townend hopes that her stories take the reader on a journey to often a dark place and only sometimes back again.

SJ won the Secret Attic short story contest (Spring 2020), has had fiction published with Sledgehammer Lit Mag, Hash Journal, Ghost Orchid Press, Bandit Fiction, Black Hare Press, Black Petals Horror Magazine, Ellipsis Zine, Gravely Unusual, Gravestone Press, Holy Flea, Horla Horror and was long listed for the Women on Writing non-fiction contest in 2020.

She has also written and self-published two dark mystery novels, both of which are available to purchase on Amazon: (Tabitha Fox Never Knocks, Twenty-Seven and the Unkindness of Crows).

Follow her on Twitter: @SJTownend